Council Grove

GLENNETTE DAY WIMMER

To my Heavenly Father

Acknowledgement

When I was a young girl of about nine or ten a desire was put into my mind to write a story about a girl in trouble. I postponed writing a story for decades until now. After much prayerful consideration, I embarked on writing this book. I want to thank my Heavenly Father for the words, imagination, energy, and skills to bring these characters into existence and tell their stories. God has provided me with help along the way and most especially from friends and associates with the skills I lacked. These important people are Susan Costello, Kay Keck, and Pam Cain. Thank you for helping me do what I believe God asked me to do many, many years ago.

Introduction

The year 1861 is remembered for the start of the Civil War leaving other historical events from that year almost forgotten. The Western Territory of Kansas celebrated becoming a state that year. Four years later many Southerners, weary from the war, looked to Kansas and other western regions for a chance to start a new life. The South had a generation of young people who had been children during the war and came of age in the first years after the war ended. This book is a collection of stories about six of Georgia's post-war adolescents who left all that was familiar to venture to the new state of Kansas.

Table of Contents

Character List

CHARACTER	DESCRIPTION
Belk Family	Family with missing daughter
Cabot (Cab) Neely	Marilyn's second husband
Catherine	Susan's stepmother
The Cochrans	Marilyn's neighbors in Juniper
Drew Watson	Ranch hand on Neely ranch
Granny Jenkins	Marilyn lived with her
Hughes Family	Marilyn grew up on their farm
Ida Mae Martin	One of four main characters
Jerry Sullins	Ranch hand on Neely ranch
Jake Edmond	Sheriff of Alma
Jenny Belk	Young girl from Alma
Joe and Bessie	Slave children that lived next to Marilyn

John & Elizabeth Gentry	Susan rode a wagon train with them to Council Grove
Joseph O'Brien	Gentleman that Susan was to marry
Junior O'Brien	Joseph O'Brien's son
Leland Martin	One of four main characters
Marilyn Woodall	One of four main characters
Martins	Parents of Leland and Ida Mae
Marty	Marilyn's and Cab's son
Mr. and Mrs. Hartley	Susan's employer, owned hotel in Council Grove
Nolans	Kansas employer of Joe and Bessie
Pappy	Organized the wagon train in Independence
Pastor Faulkner	Minister in Council Grove
Reverend Baker	Pastor at the Nashville Way Station
Reverend Brewer	Minister in Emporia
Roy Smith	Susan's first husband
Sarah	Widow that Susan helped for five days
Sheriff Walsh	Sheriff in Emporia
Sheriff Oliver	Sheriff in Council Grove
Susan Day	One of four main characters
Mrs. Woodall	Marilyn's mother

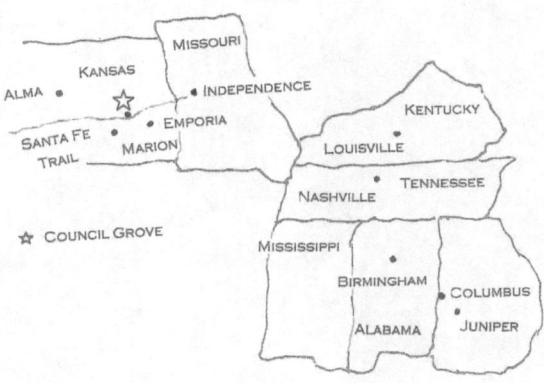

MAP OF SUSAN'S JOURNEY

In 1825, the Kaw (or Kanza) Tribe and the Osage Tribe signed treaties with the United States government allowing settlers to pass unharmed through their land on the Santa Fe Trail. The site selected for the signing of the treaties was under a grove of trees. This historical event lead to the naming of the town, Council Grove.

After Council Grove was established, another tree became significant to the town, a large oak tree was designated the "post office". Any traveler willing to deliver a message or letter left at the tree was greatly appreciated.

Council Grove became one of the last stops for supplies along the Santa Fe Trail before wagon trains set out for a long, hard journey to Santa Fe.

Susan's Story

My name is Susan Day, and I was a child during the years of the Civil War. Before the war, my hometown of Columbus, Georgia was a thriving cotton mill town that employed hundreds of men in the textile industry. Because of the flourishing economy, many small businesses sprang up and produced a sizeable middle-class. After many years of hard work, my family became one of the fortunate middle-class.

When I was a little girl my parents spent every Sunday afternoon, walking the streets of Columbus near the river and the cotton mills. I was too young to understand their motive but later learned they were seeking an affordable building to rent. All the activity around the river and the cotton mills was a perfect location for a small business, and my father's dream was to open a restaurant. At last, the Sunday walks stopped, and we settled into a two-story building a short distance from the hub of the business district. The long wait for our restaurant was worth it because the wind often blew the delicious aroma of barbeque in the direction of the mills and the river.

My family consisted of my parents and me. We lived upstairs over the restaurant as most small business owners did in those days. In the early years of the restaurant, Papa couldn't afford to pay for outside help, so all the work was done by family members. When I was too young to work my parents made a fenced off play area in the corner of the dining room so they could keep an eye on me while they cooked and served the customers. When I got to school-age, I was expected to help in the diner. Despite the hard work and long hours, we lived a comfortable life.

When I was ten years old, my mother suddenly died. Her death was hard for me to accept and even more challenging was when my father re-married the following year. My stepmother's name was Catherine. She was a widow with three little girls, ages eight, six, and three. When Catherine and the girls moved in with us, we had to do some shifting to make room for everyone and for the first time in my life, I shared my bedroom. As I got to know Catherine better, I realized she was kind, thoughtful, and slow to anger even with four girls to care for and her duties in the restaurant. She proved to be a good mother to us all, and after some time I accepted her as my mother.

In late 1860 everyday life started to change. We could feel the tension in the air; we knew the war was coming. The mills were running at full capacity. Extra men were hired, and they worked around the clock. Often customers were turned away when our kitchen was depleted of food. Our workdays grew longer than ever before, and the diners' constant talk of war made the days seem even longer.

War was declared in the spring of 1861. There were plenty of young men who volunteered for military duty, so Papa didn't concern himself with joining the army. But in the fall of 1862, the war took a different turn - the Confederate army began seeking more recruits to fill their ranks. My father decided to join the army. He reasoned, like most of the Southern men of his day, "The war won't last much longer. The South is winning, and the Yankees can't hold out much longer".

With so many men away in the war, our restaurant business was a fraction of what it had been. When Papa joined the army, he also made what he called an "enlistment plan" for the family. The plan was to temporarily close the restaurant until the war ended and for us to continue living upstairs and discourage anyone from renting the first floor. Papa wanted us to keep the restaurant property so that we could reopen our business when the war ended. He felt we could manage financially on our savings till he came home.

During Papa's time away from us, he wrote home regularly. His letters were always about his fellow soldiers and the intense suffering that they all endured from the weather, insect bites, home-sickness, and hunger. Each soldier was responsible for purchasing their personal items and shoes. When Papa wrote us about the few men without money or families to help them and how they existed without the basic things they needed it would break our hearts. Boredom was another hardship that Papa wrote about which I found difficult to believe. The men preferred fighting to waiting for the next battle, but I could understand that the endless waiting was hard on morale.

In early 1864, we received notice that the Union army captured Papa's entire regiment. He was made a prisoner of war and sent to a camp in Elmira, New York where he died of dysentery shortly after his incarceration. I had lost everyone blood related to me. All of us became a grieving family like many others around us.

After my father's death, our savings dwindled and the war escalated. Food became expensive and in short supply. Our financial situation would have been a crisis if not for our landlord's help. Our landlord offered Catherine free rent until the war ended. His generosity to us stemmed from his belief that the Yankees might think twice before they burned his building if they saw women and children living there. He feared the

Yankees would burn Columbus as they had Atlanta. He feared his empty building would be the first thing to be set ablaze if the Yankees came. He sealed off all entrances to the restaurant on the first floor and his hammering the doors shut was the third death I had to mourn. The dream of the restaurant reopening was gone just like my parents.

Catherine seized the "free rent" as a way to gain financially, and she began moving in some of her relatives to live with us. The new living arrangements meant that only adults slept in the three bedrooms, and all the children, including me, moved to pallets on the floor of the parlor. We had six adults and six children living in our home. At night, we had to walk carefully not to step on a sleeping child. We were crowded and always short of food, not to mention the lack of privacy. The little bit of rent we got from Catherine's relatives did help, but it was never enough.

Volunteer nurses were always in demand at the Columbus field hospitals. Catherine and I volunteered like many others. Sometimes the number of patients was overwhelming, especially, when we'd receive the overflow from Atlanta's hospitals. Nursing proved to be a blessing for me because it kept me busy and not focused on my losses. I couldn't feel sorry for myself when I would see the conditions of the wounded men I cared for.

We were always hungry for news about the war. I would escape our overcrowded apartment by walking to the train station every day to scout for discarded reading material. No trip to the depot was considered a waste in my opinion. Even if I didn't get any newspapers, I had a few minutes to myself.

My visits to the train depot gave me an idea of how we could make some extra money. As far back as I could remember there were always boys at the station selling peanuts to the passengers, but all those young men were gone to war now. Why couldn't a girl sell peanuts? Catherine liked my idea, and we decided to sell peanuts at the depot if we could find raw peanuts to purchase. We had the advantage of my father's list of local farmers that supplied produce for the restaurant, and we began to contact the families on Papa's list. Soon a few raw peanuts began to be delivered to the house. We would boil the peanuts at night, then package and sell them in the morning. Our little business earned me the nickname "Peanut."

One morning I was at the train depot selling peanuts as usual and keeping an eye out for something good to read when I spotted a magazine that literally stopped me in my tracks. The magazine title was *The Western Matrimonial*. I grabbed up the magazine - I'd never seen anything like it before and couldn't wait to get home to start reading. There were articles from men and women seeking courtship and marriage and for a small fee anyone could place their advertisement by writing their ad and mailing it to the magazine.

The war had left everything in such disarray that young people didn't marry and start families as they had in previous years. I wanted to marry like all girls of seventeen, but I never had an opportunity to court anyone. My priority was our financial problems not finding a husband. I showed the magazine to Catherine, and we talked about whether I should place an advertisement of my own. Catherine agreed that it was probably the best option I had for finding a husband.

The ad I mailed in was as follows:

Young, attractive, Southern girl of 17 seeks friendship and possible marriage with an eligible young man of means. I am a Christian girl that likes to cook, served as a nurse during the war, helped parents run family-owned restaurant, not opposed to traveling west, quiet, and soft-spoken.

The ad, of course, had to say attractive – all the other ads did.

Within a couple of weeks, I received a letter from a widower named Joseph O'Brien. He owned a ranch near Council Grove,

Kansas, and was 32 years old with a young son of 13. I enjoyed his letters so much! Catherine and I would read them many times to each other. He'd tell about his ranch, the cattle, and horses. He wrote me about his plans for the ranch and how he needed someone to share in those plans. It was all so romantic and uplifting to read his letters. After a few weeks of writing, he made an offer to send me travel money so that I could come to Kansas to meet him and his son. He apologized that I would have to be the one to make the trip because he was unable to leave his ranch and livestock. He'd like for us to spend some time getting to know each other better and then decide on matrimony.

Catherine was ready for me to leave the nest; she had three younger daughters to provide for. She had never said anything to me about leaving, but I could sense how she felt. So, I wrote back to Mr. O'Brien accepting his offer to come to Kansas. Within weeks a cash-filled letter arrived plus some travel instructions - the Council Grove stage was not dependable so I had to travel the last miles by covered wagon from Independence, Missouri, to Council Grove.

I immediately purchased stagecoach fare from Columbus to Nashville hoping to get another stage northwest to Independence once I reached Nashville. I packed what few things I had and took two of my mother's dresses that I had saved for a special occasion - I figured the special occasion had arrived. The recent rain and flooding had affected the availability of a northbound stage, so I had to leave for Nashville the next day. I didn't have much time for goodbyes to family and friends, but I visited my mother's grave one last time.

The stagecoach ride to Nashville was miserable, dusty, bumpy, and dirty but that was nothing compared with several of the people that shared my coach. Nights at the way station were spent avoiding drunks, scary men and foul-smelling individuals who had traveled for days without washing. Many times, the way stations didn't have enough beds and folks slept on chairs and benches. Most of the time I could find a place on the floor to stretch out, after all, that was how I had been sleeping.

Upon reaching Nashville, I discovered there wasn't another north-bound stage for five days. I really dreaded the thought of five days at the way station, because it was expensive as well as uncomfortable. On my first day of waiting, a local pastor, Reverend Baker, stopped by the station. He made a habit of visiting the station daily to spread the gospel to anyone who would listen. When he approached me, I told him I was a Christian girl traveling alone, and I had a travel dilemma. He then exclaimed, "I may have a solution to your long wait." He asked me if I'd be willing to do some domestic work for the five days in exchange for room and board with one of his church members. His parishioner's name was Sarah. She was a widow with a newborn baby, two small children, and in desperate need of help. If I did some cooking and washing for her, that would pay my room and board. I agreed, figuring nothing could have been worse than five days with the men at the way station.

Reverend Baker loaded my bag into his wagon, and we set off for Sarah's house. As we rode along, he told me about the generosity of his church and that there was a small food donation in the back of his wagon he was delivering to Sarah. I was glad to know I would be eating supper tonight. Her home was nothing more than a small cabin in need of some minor repairs on the outside, but when we got inside I couldn't believe the condition of her house and her children! Dirt everywhere, unbathed children, and everyone was hungry. All this was overwhelming, and I wasn't sure where to start. So, I started with what my parents would have done. I fixed a big meal and fed everyone. The next four days was laundry, cooking, and chopping wood all my waking hours. The last day I managed to have a couple of hours with the family to read to them and tell stories of the Old South. The children reminded me of my stepsisters and homesickness started to set in when Reverend Baker came to collect me for my return to the way station. I was headed to Independence next.

In Joseph's last letter he instructed me that once I reached Independence, I should locate an older gentleman named, Pappy, who would help me get a ride with a family in a covered wagon that would be stopping for supplies in Council Grove. It didn't take me long to locate Pappy and, much to my relief he had my arrangements made. I was to ride with John and Elizabeth Gentry in their wagon. The Gentrys were newlyweds on their way to Santa Fe and were glad to get a paying passenger at least as far as the General Store in Council Grove. Pappy telegraphed Joseph with our estimated arrival date into Council Grove, and Joseph would be at the General Store waiting for me.

I was free to explore Independence since the wagon train would not leave for a week. I spent some of my days watching Pappy dealing with an assortment of people preparing to go West. My money was lasting better than expected, so I decided to splurge on a hotel room and sleep in a bed for the first time in ages. Pappy gave me some odd jobs to help stretch my money and feed myself. My Southern accent proved to be a blessing because I never got lonely. It seems some folks had never heard a South Georgia accent and they would engage me in conversation just so they could hear me talk.

The week passed quickly. Early Monday morning, everyone preparing to leave on the Santa Fe Trail reported to Pappy and got their wagon in line. The line of wagons seemed to go on forever - a total of 27 wagons left that morning. John and Elizabeth were most agreeable people, especially Elizabeth. We talked about men and marriage all the way to Council Grove! When we would stop at night, John would sleep outside and let us ladies sleep inside the wagon which was very gracious of him. It took us about three days to reach Council Grove.

On the third day, we finally made it to the General Store at Council Grove. The Gentrys had limited time and went about their shopping as soon as we arrived. I started looking for anyone who might be Joseph, but no luck. Finally, when all the shoppers left the store, and I had finished giving my goodbyes and thanks to John and Elizabeth, I had a chance to ask the storekeeper if he knew Joseph O'Brien. He assured me he did, that Joseph owned a sizeable ranch just out from town but that he hadn't seen Joseph in town for some time. I was disappointed and tired, so I decided to get a hotel room for the night. Maybe, we had just gotten our dates confused, and all would be well in the morning.

As I was walking toward the hotel, I met the sheriff and stopped him to inquire about Joseph and told him why I was asking. I explained that I had come from Georgia as a possible Mail Order Bride and no one was waiting for me. He looked a bit puzzled by what I had told him, but I didn't press him. I was just too tired. The sheriff agreed getting a room at the hotel for the night was the best thing to do and walked with me to the hotel. The sheriff said to the desk clerk "Charge this little lady's room and supper to Mr. O'Brien. O'Brien should pay for his tardy behavior." Before leaving me that evening, the sheriff suggested that he could borrow a buggy in the morning to drive me out to the ranch if Joseph did not show, perhaps something at the ranch was keeping him. I could not thank him enough for his generous offer.

After I freshened up in my hotel room, I headed to the dining room on the first floor. I had a hardy meal and spent a few minutes in conversation with the owner, Mr. Hartley. I told him about my parent's restaurant before the war, and he was delighted to have someone to talk "shop" with. He asked me to return to the dining room just before closing time so that I could meet his wife and we'd have dessert and coffee. I made sure I returned promptly at closing time for dessert. The Hartleys and I visited for a couple of hours and discussed the headaches of running a restaurant. I even shared with them how I got the nickname, "Peanut." The Hartleys loved my peanut story so much that they started to call me by my nickname as well. The Hartleys reminded me so much of my parents, and I went to sleep that night with thoughts about my wonderful evening with them.

The next morning, I was having breakfast in the hotel dining room when I noticed the sheriff with a buggy parked just outside the hotel. I thought he was rushing to judgment on Joseph's timing of coming into town but thought I best go along with his plan. I quickly gathered my things from my room and left with the sheriff for the O'Brien ranch. When I arrived at the ranch, it was everything Joseph had said it was. There was activity everywhere I looked except for the house which was usually quiet. The sheriff told me to wait in the buggy while he checked the house to see if anyone was in. Then a few minutes later he reappeared in the doorway saying you can come in now and meet Mr. O'Brien.

The sheriff helped me out of the buggy and set my bag on the front porch. I couldn't help thinking to myself "This is odd, why didn't he take my bag inside the house?" He explained to me that Joseph had been under the weather for a few days, so please excuse Joseph's appearance. I said "Of course" and made my way into the bedroom to find a grey-headed, wrinkled, old man of 50 or 60 years of age who was obviously very sick. The sheriff asked, "Do you want to stay or go back to town?" I replied, "I will stay. It looks like Joseph could use some help." I thought to myself that I owe this man a great deal for paying my way from Georgia, and it wouldn't be right to leave someone so sick and needing help.

Not really knowing what to do, I did what came natural, I cooked. When I got some soup ready, I fed Joseph and he began to gain enough strength to feel up to a conversation. I asked about his son, Junior, and he told me that Junior and some of his friends had gone hunting for a few days. Joseph confessed that he'd not told the truth in his letters about their ages - he was 55 years old, and his son was 18. He figured that if he'd been honest about his age in his letters, no young woman would have considered him.

It appeared the only lie he told me was about his and his son's age. The ranch was just as he described it. I went on with the nursing and household duties that seemed to be so urgent and the days went by quickly. I didn't have time to think of much except my chores and gratitude to Joseph for paying my way to Kansas. I was enjoying a degree of comfort that I had not known since I was a child - a warm bed and all I could eat. Money didn't appear to be a problem either. Joseph always said, "Get what you want from town and send a ranch hand to fetch it."

Joseph told me that he had promoted one of his ranch hands to foreman so that he could slow down due to his age. As the weeks went by, we had gotten to know each other better, and the awkwardness of our relationship had passed. One evening I decided to confront Joseph about his health since he wasn't improving - if anything he was getting weaker. Joseph began to share with me that he had other health problems besides just getting older. His doctor had diagnosed him with some form of blood disorder and said that he had less than a year to live. His doctor told him that in his last days he would need someone like a nurse with him because he'd be too weak to care for himself. The doctor advised getting someone lined up for when the time came.

He stressed to me that he was financially set for life but lacked finding someone to care for him. The problem was a shortage of women. All the respectable women around Council Grove were married with families of their own to care for and most saloon girls couldn't be counted on - they just wanted a man's money.

He'd heard stories of men finding good wives in the Mail Order magazines, so he started reading advertisements in the *Western Matrimonial* hoping to find someone suitable. My ad caught his attention when I said I was a nurse during the war. He could tell that I had a couple of years of nursing experience and probably had seen men in worse shape than any disease he had. He jokingly said that being a cook was a plus, too. He started to write to me and liked what he'd found. When he made the money offer to come to Kansas, and I didn't take the money and run he knew I was honest. He'd found his nurse!

He went on to say that because of his health he was not prepared to marry me or anyone else. He hoped that I would come to know Junior and consider marriage to him. After all, Junior and I were close in age, and he felt that Junior might settle down if he got to know a good woman. I was horrified! How could anyone be so manipulative and deceitful? I couldn't believe I let someone take advantage of me to this degree! I stormed out of his room and headed for the porch to cool off.

When I reached the porch, I couldn't help noticing the most beautiful sunset despite everything I had just heard and the anger burning in me. Sunsets were special to my parents, and they taught me to count my blessings when I gazed at a beautiful sunset. I wanted to calm down, and I tried to remember some scripture from the Bible that would comfort me, but I couldn't remember anything. Later that evening I began to calm down some and gain a thankful attitude. I began to thank God for keeping me safe through the war and for a kind and loving stepmother when I lost my parents. God had kept me safe during the trip to Kansas and led me to Joseph – a kind and generous man. My prayers made me realize I had only thought of myself and what was to become of me. I had given no thought to God's plan, only mine. I spent a long time on the porch praying and asking for His will in this matter. Peace finally came to me late into the night. I peeked into Joseph's room and found him sleeping soundly, and I retired as well.

The next morning, I brought Joseph his breakfast and told him I had forgiven him for deceiving me and understood what it was like to be in dire need. I assured him that I would stay at the ranch until his passing and see that he had a proper funeral and a Christian burial to put his concerns to rest. I could see relief all over his face.

Nursing duties consumed my time, and I was now at peace. I knew what God wanted me to do. During the war, there was so little anyone could do for the dying soldiers other than keeping them as comfortable as possible. The nurses turned their focus to the spiritual needs of the dying men. They would read comforting Bible verses to their patients and attempt to lead the unsaved to Christ before their passing. So that's what I did for Joseph.

Joseph was getting weaker every day, and we decided to start making his final arrangements. Joseph was agreeable to having Pastor Faulkner from Council Grove come to the house to help with the planning, so I sent word to the doctor on one of his visits to ask Pastor Faulkner to stop in.

The next day the pastor came. Joseph and Pastor Faulkner talked for nearly an hour behind his closed bedroom door. When Pastor Faulkner emerged from his room he announced, "Joseph would like to go over the funeral arrangements now." We all three huddled and discussed hymns and scripture for the funeral. As we wrapped up our conversation, Joseph told me that he had made a contribution to the church and given his funeral expense money to Pastor Faulkner for safe keeping since Junior was not trustworthy with money. Pastor Faulkner would release the money to me when I needed it to pay his final expenses. I was pleased that Joseph trusted me that much.

Just as Pastor Faulkner was leaving, our peaceful visit was interrupted by a loud, disruptive, red-faced young man screaming "Stop! Stop!" The intruder was Junior, the son I had not met. Junior was in town and overheard the doctor sending a preacher to the house. Junior took the pastor's visit to the ranch to mean a marriage ceremony was going to take place and he was going to lose his inheritance to some "South Georgia Mail Order Bride." We all burst out laughing, and Pastor Faulkner assured him he had come for a visit, not a wedding. Junior left, and I didn't see him again for days.

The next week Joseph died peacefully in his sleep. I asked the foreman to go into town to find Junior and bring the undertaker. Junior came straight away, and I explained to him the terms of the agreement that Joseph and I had and that I would leave the ranch after Joseph was laid to rest beside his mother. Junior was happy to know that I would not be a problem for him. I couldn't help wondering how the ranch would fare with Joseph gone and Junior in charge.

The funeral service was held in the parlor of Joseph's house, and Pastor Faulkner presided as planned. There was a large gathering of people, neighbors, ranch hands, shopkeepers, and business associates that attended his funeral. The sheriff and the Hartleys also came, and I was so glad to see folks I actually knew. After the burial, I began to tell the Hartleys goodbye and thank them for coming, when they suggested that I come back into town with them and spend the night at the hotel, their treat. They insisted that I had no other reason to be at the ranch and no one was sure how Junior would be acting - best to stay clear of him. I agreed, packed my bag, and left with the Hartleys.

That evening at the hotel the Hartleys offered me a job with room and board at the hotel. I could not believe their offer! I accepted it immediately.

Pastor Faulkner stopped by the hotel a few days after Joseph's death to deliver the final expense money that he had kept in safe keeping. He told me that I would find several hundred dollars extra in the money that he had been holding. Joseph had left me some money so that I wouldn't be destitute when he died.

I was soon known all over Council Grove as the "Mail Order Nurse" who moved in with the Hartleys. My hotel job didn't end my nursing days as I was often sought to help the sick if the Hartleys could spare me.

Marilyn's Story

My name is Marilyn Woodall. I was born in 1850, the daughter of a sharecropper. We lived and worked on the Hughes farm in Juniper, Georgia. Pa liked to brag that we were the second generation of Woodalls to sharecrop for Mr. Hughes. As I grew older and learned more about the world, I realized just how poor we were and certainly didn't seek to be a third-generation sharecropper's wife.

Mrs. Hughes had three boys just a few years older than me, so I always had "big brothers" when I needed one. I was the only girl on the farm as well as my parent's only child. I was a bit spoiled and catered to by everyone.

Our closest neighbor was the Cochran farm. The Cochrans were an exception to the norm from the rest of the farmers in the area because they had two slaves. Mr. Cochran saved someone's life once and was given two slave children as a gift of gratitude. At the time of the gift, no information about the children was given such as their names, ages or if they were blood relatives. Mrs. Cochran named them, Joe and Bessie. Their estimated ages were somewhere between the youngest Hughes boy (thirteen) and me (ten). Since Mrs. Cochran, a strict Southern Baptist, didn't know if Joe and Bessie were blood-related to each other she insisted they marry each other when they came of age. She would always say, "We can't have Joe and Bessie living in sin." The Cochrans were good to them in some ways - by that I mean they were well fed and not beaten, but they were slaves and had no choices in their lives. After they were married, the Cochrans had a small cabin built near their house for them to live in. For unknown reasons, Bessie never had any children.

Several of the men in Juniper engaged in a variety of sports activities, but Mr. Cochran was an avid hunter, and he insisted on Joe going with him on his hunting trips. Joe learned from one of the best, and he shared the same enthusiasm for hunting that Mr. Cochran did. During the winter months, Mr. Cochran and Joe provided meat, mostly venison, to needy people in the community. That's how I came to be friends with Joe and Bessie. We were one of those needy families.

In 1859, the talk of a Civil War started and life as we had always known it began to change. The cotton mills in the nearby town of Columbus were advertising for production workers. The cotton mills stepped up production to meet the demands for supplies for the Confederate Army, and they were hiring every man they could get. Many of Juniper's families (mine included) jumped at a chance to be employed in the cotton mills rather than the backbreaking work of farming and quickly moved to Columbus to find jobs.

At first, Papa enjoyed the easier pace of the cotton mill, and he especially enjoyed the company of his co-workers. On paydays they would treat themselves to lunch at a popular place called the Day's Restaurant. It was a little family owned diner that catered to the mill workers. On one of those occasions, Papa saw a sign in the window – "Wanted Kitchen help, Apply Inside." He knew this would be the perfect place for Mama to work if he could convince her. After much coaxing from Papa, she reluctantly agreed to at least apply for the job. The next morning Mama set out for the restaurant with me in tow. To our surprise, she was hired on the spot and put straight to work. When Mr. Day had finished talking with Mama about her duties, he took a good look at me and put me to work as well!

The afternoon of our first day of work at the restaurant was when I met, Susan Day, the owner's daughter. Susan was the same age as me and we became instant friends. Susan's parents had put her to work in the kitchen at a young age, and I figured that's why Mr. Day hired me too. Susan and I did everything together – we worked in the restaurant around our school hours and played whenever we could get away from the grownups. Susan became my best friend.

Even though Papa left Juniper to go work in Columbus, he stayed in touch with Mr. Hughes, and they remained friends for life. Besides owning a farm in Juniper, Mr. Hughes also operated a sawmill in Columbus that he inherited from his father-in-law. He wasn't especially fond of the lumber business, but his three sons preferred the lumber business over the farm. So, Mr. Hughes kept the sawmill for his boys to take over one day and split his time between the farm and the sawmill.

Papa would visit the sawmill when Mr. Hughes was in town. After a few months, Papa grew to dislike his job at the mill and during one of his visits with Mr. Hughes he expressed how much he hated working inside all day. Papa complained that the lack of sunlight wasn't natural and was making him sick. Mr. Hughes was delighted to know he didn't like the cotton mill and quickly responded with a job offer at the sawmill. Papa gladly accepted his offer.

A few months after Papa started working at the sawmill the war began, and all three of Mr. Hughes' sons enlisted in the army. The war had created a shortage of young men in the Columbus area which left Mr. Hughes and Papa as the only employees at the sawmill. They had to work long and exhausting hours to keep up with demand. As the war went on the army started recruiting older men, and Papa saw the military as a graceful way out of the sawmill job. He enlisted.

Every family was affected by the war in some way. Mr. Hughes was forced to close the sawmill and went back to farming. Mrs. Hughes died from what we believe was a broken heart when her boys left for war. Mr. Day enlisted in the army, closed his business, and all his employees were laid off. Mama and I didn't have a job anymore which lead to financial problems. Then the worst happened, just before the war ended Papa died from wounds he received in battle.

When Mr. Hughes learned of Papa's death, he insisted that Mama and I move back to the farm with him until the war was over. Mama felt we'd be safe with Mr. Hughes and she quickly moved us back to Juniper. Life on the farm was boring for me without Susan around. There was just the three of us. Mr. Hughes spent most of his day napping and letting Mama wait on him. There was always housework to keep us busy as we tried to undo the years the house had sat without a good cleaning. We both worked to make Mr. Hughes as comfortable as possible so that we'd have a place to live.

Walking about the farm, exploring the pastures and fields were my only entertainment. One day I came to the overgrown fence that separated the Hughes farm from the Cochran farm. I cleared the vines and vegetation and climbed over. I could see Joe's and Bessie's cabin in the distance. As a child, I remembered playing with them and the fun we had. I ran most of the way to their cabin only to find them out in the fields working - I should have known they'd be working in the daytime. If I would get to see them, I'd have to come back after dark.

When night finally came, and Mama went to sleep, I sneaked out of the house, making a straight shot for Bessie's cabin. It was difficult getting to their house in the dark even in the moonlight, but I made it to their door. Joe and Bessie cautiously opened their door in disbelief that it was really me at their door knocking. Our visit was short because I was so nervous about getting caught sneaking out of the house, but I promised to come back soon. While I was with them, Joe and Bessie had asked me lots of questions about the war and what was going to happen to them when the war ended.

Now I had something to focus on! I started collecting newspaper articles about the war, and I would read them to Joe and Bessie on my nightly visits. When I didn't have war news, I would read my letters from Susan to them. As time went on, I told my mother that I was going over to the Cochrans to check on them. The Cochrans were elderly, and Mama thought I was kind and thoughtful - now I didn't have to sneak around anymore to see Joe and Bessie.

Once, I asked Joe and Bessie "Why don't you just leave; the Cochrans are too old to stop you?" They told me that they had talked about leaving but where would they go? They didn't know anything about money except you have to have it, and would they be considered runaway slaves? That's when I started reading to them about the Great American West and how so many people were going West to get free farmland. That became their favorite stories.

After the war ended Mr. Hughes, Mama and I did as much farming as we could manage but it was a lot of hard work. Mr. Hughes had lost all three sons in the war and had no reason to keep the sawmill any longer, so he sold it. He continued to let Mama wait on him, and she was happy with the arrangement. Mama was determined to stay on with Mr. Hughes as his housekeeper.

When we moved back to the farm in Juniper, I wasn't able to see Susan very often, but we stayed in touch by mail. A couple of years after the war, she had written telling me about a gentleman in Kansas that she was corresponding with. I couldn't wait for her next letter to hear more about her gentleman friend. After waiting months, I received a letter from her postmarked from Kansas! Her letter updated me on how she had left Georgia by stagecoach and gone to Kansas to marry as a mail-order bride. The marriage never took place, and she ended up working in a hotel in Council Grove, Kansas. She also wrote to ask if I'd like to come to Kansas and join her. We could work in the hotel restaurant just like old times. She also told me about the abundance of available young men! She went on to say, not to worry about money. If I wanted to come, she would send me the money to make the trip. I couldn't get Susan's letter out of my mind!

That evening I read Susan's letter to Bessie and Joe and told them I had made my decision to leave home and join Susan. That's when Joe suggested that all three of us go. From then on, we began to plan how we would make such a trip. In Susan's next letter she sent us as much information as she could remember. She told us we'd have to wait till Spring rain and floods had ended and she'd send maps of the trails and roads her stagecoach used. We planned to travel the same roads as the stage lines but in a wagon. Joe insisted on a strong, young mule and a good wagon. We could haul our provisions in the wagon, and he'd trap small game along the way to supplement our rations. We all three agreed to his plan, but telling Mr. Cochran and my mother was going to be the problem.

The Cochrans expected Joe and Bessie to leave after the war was over. But my mother refused to hear anything about me leaving for Kansas and especially with two recently freed slaves. Mr. Hughes started to accept the idea of my leaving and began giving us advice like how to keep our food safe from predators at night – things that would never occur to me. After weeks of waiting Susan's money arrived. Mr. Hughes wanted to pick out the mule we purchased, and he gave us a used but sturdy wagon from his sawmill days. He made sure we had a canvas cover to use when it rained. We started to gather our supplies and wait for the weather to improve when Mr. Hughes made one more suggestion. He brought out an old shotgun and gave the three of us shooting lessons. He convinced Mama that we would be better off with a gun and know how to use it than go out at the mercy of the world. Finally, in early May the weather turned nice, and it was time to start out for Kansas. I had to confront my mother again that nothing was going to stop me and I didn't want to leave on a bad note. She finally came around like she always did and we had a good farewell.

It took us three long months to reach Kansas. If I had known how hard it was going to be, I would never have left home. I didn't realize how bad it was till we reached Tennessee. By that time, I was so exhausted I rode in the back of the wagon for days, unable to lift my head. At that point, we had come too far to turn back for home and still had a lot more miles ahead of us. What was so discouraging in Tennessee was when we saw the horizon getting higher and higher and we grew wearier – even the mule! The mule had lost a good bit of weight, and so had we. Joe and Bessie had reached exhaustion now. We were afraid if we lost our mule that we'd not survive. So, we let the mule graze, and all of us rested. It was good that we did rest for a while because we had a hard time going over the mountains with the wagon – we were forced to walk many times to lighten the load on the wagon.

After surviving mountains, next was surviving rivers to cross and insect bites, but we just kept going. I wrote to Susan and Mama frequently and posted the letters when we would go into town for more supplies. Joe was good at trapping and kept us in fresh meat, mostly rabbits and squirrels. Our money lasted even though we were down to our last dollars when we reached Council Grove.

We got some odd looks and questions when people would see a white girl with two ex-slaves. We had some fun with them. We'd tell made up stories about who we were and where we were headed just to see the expressions on their faces. For the most part, everyone was civil and paid no attention to us.

As we walked or rode along, we had "school." We would recite the alphabet, multiplication tables, addition, and anything else we could do while we traveled. At night, our school tablets became sticks and the dirt around the dim light from the campfire. Somewhere north of Tennessee is where Joe and Bessie learned to write their names. We all three got firsthand knowledge of geography and how to manage money. When all our other subjects got too boring, we had discussions about history and politics, but with our limited education, the discussions did not last very long.

We practically collapsed on the porch of the Hartley Hotel when we finally reached Council Grove. We rested for several days from our journey and then started our new jobs. Mr. Hartley had gotten Joe and Bessie employment on the Nolan farm near Council Grove. All of us went out to meet the Nolans and see where Joe and Bessie would be living and working. Everyone agreed the mule and wagon should stay with Joe and Bessie to give them the freedom to go as they pleased.

Susan and I had settled into a routine of work at the hotel and restaurant. We didn't get to spend much time together because of our shifts. One worked while the other was off. On some of my free Sunday afternoons, I would visit with Joe and Bessie. If I went out to the Nolan farm, I'd have to go alone because Susan would be working or nursing someone or at church. When winter came, I didn't venture out from the hotel because of the cold. I wasn't accustomed to severe weather since this was my first winter after leaving Georgia's warm climate. The cold, dark days of winter began to wear on me, and I grew discontent and bored

24

with life at the hotel. My feelings reached a point of extreme jealousy of Susan. Susan was always the Hartleys favored one, and the doctor was always bragging on Susan when she would do some nursing for him. I felt forgotten and alone. I had not made any new friends, and the guests at the hotel didn't make for long friendships.

If I had a choice about working the hotel or the restaurant, I always picked the restaurant because I'd get to meet more people and have a little time to chat with the customers when they'd pay their checks. One particular day I started conversing with a young man named Roy Smith while he paid his check. He was well dressed, handsome and a bit flirty but I didn't really mind the flirting – I liked it. He wanted to see me after work, and from there we began to spend time together, and then after a couple of weeks, he proposed to me. It was a whirlwind romance for sure, but I accepted his marriage proposal.

When I told Susan and the Hartleys about my engagement, I was met with instant disapproval. Everyone said that we had not known each other long enough, that he appeared to be a drifter, not to rush into anything. Their criticism only made me more anxious to run away and marry Roy. I complained to Roy that everyone was against our marriage. He suggested that we forget about them, marry early next Saturday morning, and leave for Emporia as soon as the ceremony was over.

Roy asked if I would mind a part honeymoon and part working week in Emporia. Roy was in the freight business and was expecting a big shipment into Emporia next week. He explained that he'd have to leave Council Grove by Saturday at the latest to be in Emporia in time for his freight job and he didn't want to go without me. Roy even suggested that we borrow the mule and wagon from Joe. We could use the wagon to make even more money on his special freight delivery. Roy said he wanted to use the extra money to repay Susan the travel money she had sent me. We could give Susan her money and return the mule and wagon in a few weeks when we went back to Council Grove. Maybe that would make him acceptable to Susan. Roy had everything planned, so I quit my job at the hotel, got the wagon and mule from Joe and packed my bags.

Susan and I had a big argument the night before I married Roy. I told her she was jealous because she didn't have someone interested in her and that she didn't want to see me happy. I accused her of being an old maid that didn't know how to do anything but work and go to church, that she would never have any fun or adventure in her life because of her homely personality. Susan got really mad and told me to never come back to see her - that our friendship was over. That's how we ended a lifelong friendship.

Roy and I married that following Saturday morning and left town for the two-day journey to Emporia. Our wedding night was nothing to envy as we had to camp out just off the road near a creek. Roy insisted on exercising his husband's rights on our wedding night despite the crude sleeping arrangements. Fortunately, we had a lot of privacy in the trees.

The next morning, we made a campfire and cooked our breakfast. As soon as we finished eating Roy hitched up the mule and loaded our things into the wagon. He insisted that I go down to the creek to wash one of his shirts. I did as he asked and walked to the water. As I began scrubbing his shirt, I heard the mule's hooves and the wagon moving. I didn't think much about it at first until I realized the sounds were moving farther away from our campsite. I dropped everything and ran to see what was going on. Then I saw Roy in the wagon with his horse tied to the back of the wagon, whipping the mule, and screaming for him to 'git up'! He was racing away and leaving me behind! I ran after him, screaming for him to wait but he just kept going as if he was in a race for his life. I ran after him until I was exhausted and could run no further. I was so confused about what had just happened and why had Roy left me? I was alone on the road with nothing around me but woods, no houses, or barns nearby, just total isolation. I walked back to our campsite and waited for a bit hoping Roy would come back for me. Several hours went by, and he didn't return. No one came down the road either. I was still all alone.

I had a lot of time to think, and I started to remember Susan and the Hartleys warning me about Roy. I got up and began to look at what few things Roy had left behind - my bag with my clothes were still sitting on the ground where it had been unloaded from the wagon the night before. My handbag was laying in the dirt, and half opened, and all the money I had saved while I worked for the Hartleys was gone! I was penniless and deserted! I cried for a long time but then came to my senses that I best do something before dark. I had to find some shelter and food. I picked up my bag and started walking down the road in the direction that Roy had gone. I reasoned that I was closer to Emporia than Council Grove and maybe I would find a farmhouse or barn in which to spend the night.

I walked for several hours when my feet began to blister, I stopped, took off my shoes and continued walking barefoot. Fortunately, I didn't walk barefoot too long before a couple in a wagon came along and stopped to ask if I needed help. I burst out in tears and told them what had happened to me that my husband had left me deserted along the side of the road. They loaded me into their wagon and insisted that they take me at once to the sheriff in Emporia. I agreed and collapsed in the back of their wagon. I was so exhausted and must have napped on the way into town because it seemed like we arrived at the sheriff's office in just a few minutes. I told my story to Sheriff Walsh about being a newlywed and being deserted along the road and how my money was gone. I told the sheriff that the mule and wagon belonged to me and that Roy had taken that as well. Sheriff Walsh suggested I stay with a local widow until we got things sorted out. I was very grateful to have someone take me in and agreed to go. Just before dark Sheriff Walsh dropped me off at a little shanty that was the home of Granny Jenkins.

Granny promptly fixed me a plate of lukewarm beans for my supper. I was hungry - I had not eaten since breakfast. She made me a small pallet on the floor near the fireplace to sleep. We talked for a short while, mostly about what had happened to me, and then turned in for the night. I did manage to sleep some that first night, but the nights afterward I spent crying or lying awake wondering how I could have been so stupid.

About mid-morning of my second day with Granny, Sheriff Walsh stopped by to tell me that Roy had been seen in Emporia about noon the previous day and that he had sold the wagon and mule to the livery stable owner. After selling the wagon, he left town. It was my word against Roy about who owned the mule and wagon. The Sheriff was quick to point out that since we were married, all my property was my husband's property, so Roy wasn't guilty of stealing the wagon and mule. Susan and I had broken off our friendship over Roy, and now I had lost the mule and wagon that meant freedom for Joe and Bessie.

Sheriff Walsh also told me that Roy had been in Emporia a year or so back with another wife and he deserted her almost in the same place. Roy had taken all her money and left her beside the road while he rode off. So, am I really married to Roy? How could I find the other Mrs. Roy Smith if she was still alive or know if she had died? Kansas was a new state, and public records were hit or miss at best. Then, Granny asked me if there was any chance I could be with child. My heart stopped – yes, there was a chance. I'd have to wait and see if I had yet another problem caused by Roy.

Granny and I got along well in her little house. I tried to do as many chores as I could to earn my keep. Granny didn't seem to mind having a houseguest, and she shared her meager allotment of beans and coffee with me.

Granny was a pack-rat on a huge scale. She had a lot, and I mean a lot of clothes in her little shanty. She had a great assortment of men's clothes in all sizes, the same with children's clothes. What fascinated me the most were dresses that looked like a saloon girl's outfit. What was Granny doing with saloon girl dresses? I finally had to ask her where did you get all these clothes and why?

Granny told me that her late husband had been an undertaker back in Wichita and when he died she moved to Emporia to live with her sister. Granny and her sister supported themselves as seamstresses. When her sister died several years ago, Granny continued living in her sister's house and continued her seamstress work. Granny would wash and mend any used garments that she felt she could sell to the general stores and that gave her some money to live on. "Well, that's a clever idea, Granny, but where do you get the clothes from that you mend?" I asked. She answered, "Oh, that's the easy part, child." Granny went on to tell me how her husband had been an undertaker all his life and that he and Granny would take clothes from the dearly departed if there was no family to notice what the deceased was wearing at the cemetery. They reasoned that the dead wouldn't be needing any clothing but the living would! Granny would be sure not to refurbish and sell anything that might be recognized by the departed person's family, so she just kept the items for several years. Luckily when she moved to Emporia, she didn't have to be so careful about anyone recognizing the clothing.

The shock of Roy and now this last development with Granny being a clothing thief was a lot for me to take in but I didn't have much choice but to continue being Granny's live-in seamstress. I was thankful for a roof over my head, food in my stomach and I wasn't pregnant. I tried to find work in Emporia, but no jobs or no one wanted to hire me - I was never sure which.

The thing I found fascinating about sewing is it gives a person a lot of time to do some soul searching and reflect on their life. I had never been a spiritual person. When I was growing up, I went to church because Mama made me. But now I felt a great need for religion in my life, and I wanted to start going to church. Granny helped me find a neighbor that would pick me up on Sunday mornings, so I didn't have to walk into town for church services. Granny let me use her husband's old Bible. I would read the Bible every day and especially the handwritten notes in the margins. She also found some old sermons in a notebook that helped me understand the Bible more. Soon I was going to church every Wednesday night and twice on Sunday. My faith became everything to me.

My pastor had recently preached a message about everyone having God-given talents and gifts and that our job was to discover those talents and use them for the work of the Kingdom. That sermon resonated with me. I had been taking in laundry to make a little money for myself, but I knew that wasn't my talent. My gift was cooking. I just needed help finding a job.

I felt enough friendship with the pastor and his wife that I could go to them to ask for help in procuring employment. Rev. Brewer agreed to help me and suggested that I write up several advertisements something like this:

Experienced Cook seeks immediate hire
Strong, healthy woman of good moral character
Interested persons, please contact
Reverend Brewer
First Baptist Church
Emporia, Kansas

At Rev. Brewer's suggestion, he mailed my advertisements with his letters going to churches in the area, and he'd ask in his letters for each church to publicly post my ad. His suggestion saved me a lot of money on postage. He also added that since I didn't have a father or brother, he'd like to interview my potential employers first. My optimism soared! Within a few weeks, several letters had gone out, and I patiently waited for replies.

Cabot Neely (everyone called him Cab) owned a modest ranch near Marion, Kansas. Cab had two good ranch hands, Drew and Jerry, but they were far from cooks. A recent bout of food poisoning had all three men down for a week. Cab vowed on his next trip to Emporia, "I'm coming home with a cook!" Finally, a warm, spring day arrived, and Cab hitched his mule team to his wagon and headed to Emporia for supplies. On the top of his supply list was "A COOK." The store clerk at the Emporia General Store had recently posted an advertisement for a cook requested by Reverend Brewer. Cab read the notice quickly and made his way to the church to see Rev. Brewer. Cab noticed the ad said woman but figured she was an older lady, probably a widow.

Rev. Brewer interviewed Cab, and upon meeting his approval, offered to take him to meet the woman needing a job. Within the hour, Rev. Brewer and Cab was knocking on Granny's front door and welcomed inside. Rev. Brewer introduced everyone and proceeded to tell Cab "Marilyn is the lady advertising for a cook's job." Cab was stunned and speechless for a few seconds and then said, "I didn't expect someone this young." Cab went on to say, "I don't think this will work, having a young woman living in the same cabin with three men." Cab continued "I have two ranch hands that also live and work at the ranch. I don't have a bunkhouse, we all sleep in one room."

Rev. Brewer spoke up and reminded all of us that in Jesus's time many people lived and slept in one small room. I finally got

31

the courage to speak and said to Cab "Please give me a chance. If it doesn't work out, I promise to leave and not make any trouble for you." Cab thought for a while and finally said, "OK, I can agree to that. I'll pick you up just after sun up in the morning."

Granny and I had a good breakfast ready for Cab so that he'd know I actually could cook. Telling Granny goodbye was so hard. She gave me the Bible and sermons I had been reading at her house. I cried when I left her. I couldn't thank her enough for all she had done. Cab and I started the long journey to his ranch. We rode along not saying more than a few words on the way to his ranch. My mind was spinning with memories of my past and not knowing my future. It was nightfall when we got to the ranch. Two men came running out of the cabin when we pulled up. One of them shouted "Good grief, Cab; I thought you was gonna get us a cook, not a woman." Cab turned angrily and barked back at him, "She's our cook and a lady, and I expect her to be treated as such. Do you understand me?" He immediately got two "Yes sirs."

Cab quickly introduced the two, Jerry Sullins and Drew Watson and insisted they start unloading the wagon. I wandered into the small cabin and made my inspection. There was limited privacy, and I could see how the food poisoning was possible. Everything needed a good scrubbing. We made a curtain from a blanket to separate my bunk from the "men's quarters" and began our life together in the cramped, little cabin.

All three of the men were quite curious about my past, and I kept no secrets about what all had happened to me. I told them everything all the way back to my childhood days in Georgia, Bessie and Joe coming with me to Kansas, working with Susan at the hotel, and then the big story about Roy and how Granny helped me get back on my feet. I told them about my faith and how my prideful ways had brought destruction to me and how truly sorry I was. After that Drew, Jerry and Cab seemed to have a lot of respect for me and we became like a family, caring for each other.

Drew and Jerry were a pleasure to cook for. They made a big deal over getting a good meal. I never knew what Cab was thinking. He was a man of few words, but I do know he ate every bite I served to him. When I asked if we could say grace at our meals, Cab's reply was "By all means but don't expect me to say it."

Sundays were always a special day. I tried to cook something besides our usual fare and then after dinner we all napped and rested. Sunday afternoons gave me a chance to get away from the cabin and explore the ranch. Our little community had a small church with a minister who came every four weeks, and Cab made sure I got to church.

Gradually Drew and Jerry joined me in my nightly Bible study. On the Sundays that I didn't go to church, I made up a worship service for us. We'd sing a few hymns and read one of the sermons that came from the notebook Granny gave me. We often got into discussions about the sermon or Bible verses. Cab never participated, but he was always listening to us.

One of my favorite memories was our first Christmas. I wanted to surprise the men with a Christmas tree. I figured no one had ever decorated the cabin for Christmas and it was about time. I waited for the perfect day when they wouldn't be home for the mid-day meal, and that would give me all the time I needed to fetch the tree and get it inside. I planned to start as soon as everyone left for the day, saddle one of the mules and ride out to a tree I had found weeks earlier. The pre-selected tree appeared to be a perfect size and easy to cut down. The part of the plan where everyone left for the day went well. Saddling the mule was difficult, but I managed. My trouble started when I had to carry the ax and ride the mule at the same time. I couldn't get on the mule and hold the ax without the ax banging into the mule or me. I finally got the idea to put the ax in an old flour sack and tie it to the horn of the saddle. I rode out to my selected tree and got it chopped down, but it was a lot more tree than I thought it was. I was exhausted, it was getting late, and I needed to get home to start supper. Every time I got near the mule with the tree, it spooked him, and it was all I could do to keep him from running off. I got so frustrated with that animal I used some rope to tie half his body (his tail, front leg, back leg, and his head) to nearby trees. After tying up the mule, I was able to secure the Christmas tree to the saddle. Next, I carefully untied the mule's body parts from the trees and the mule, and I walked home. Everyone got a good laugh about my tree story that night while we threaded popcorn to decorate the tree. The tree was worth the effort. The smell and the beauty of the tree lasted for days.

I always had an abundance of flour sacks that I repurposed for our needs. I used straw and flour sacks to make an angel for the top of our tree. I pieced together enough flour sacks to make a primitive tablecloth for Christmas dinner. Our gift exchange was just a few pieces of candy, but it was like gold to us.

After a few months, I got brave enough to ask Cab to buy us a milk cow. I couldn't believe it, but he went to a lot of trouble and expense to get one. The extra milk made a big difference in our diets. We had milk and butter every day. Many times, we had extra milk that we didn't use, so I kept experimenting with the excess milk hoping I would get the knack of making cheese.

After my success with the cow request, I asked for a fenced-in vegetable garden. I got that too. It took the men away from ranch work for a few days, but the garden proved to be a blessing for year-round vegetables.

Cab sweetened his opinion of the dairy cow and the garden when we had a surplus he could sell in town. Soldiers from surrounding forts would pay top dollar for our milk and produce.

Cab was always about making money. Once Cab rode out to meet a wagon train passing through, and he sold milk and butter to them. He used the extra money to buy a set of china dishes from one of the wagons. The wagon owner was trying to lighten his load, and he sold his wife's china dishes to Cab. Cab knew how much I hated our tin plates and cups.

I had been writing my mother regularly, but I had not been entirely truthful with her about Roy. Rather than tell her that he had deserted me, I told her he had been killed in an accident at the freight office when some boxes fell on him. Roy was dead to me, so that's how I justified my lie. I picked up the truth again in my letters when I went to live with Granny. I knew it was wrong to lie, but I couldn't bring myself to tell my mother what had really happened. I loved my mother, and I just couldn't cause her to worry any more than I already had.

Feelings of guilt about my relationship with Susan began to weigh on me. Finally, I got the courage to write to Susan to see if she had forgiven me for all the hateful things I had said to her. My letter was full of apologies, but I also wanted her to know that she was right about Roy, that God had used Roy's cruelty to lead me to Christ, and that I had my life back on track. I wanted her to know that I was happy and had secured a good position. A few weeks later I received a reply from Susan, and she had forgiven me. We started our friendship up again.

The months went by, and it was Spring again. A year had passed, and all that time I had faithfully saved my pay to get legal help with an annulment. Cab promised me that when I had enough money, he'd take me to Emporia to get my legal affairs in order. In hopes I had enough money, we made the trip to Emporia only to find the district judge out of town and not due back for weeks. Reluctantly I paid an attorney to handle my case when the judge returned. I was so disappointed by the outcome of the day, but at least I had the wheels in motion. I prayed for patience.

About six weeks after the visit with the attorney, I received a letter from him that contained my official Divorce Decree....
I was a free woman at last! Cab, Drew, and Jerry helped me celebrate that evening when I showed them my letter and divorce document. Cab seemed a little quiet, I thought but, Drew and Jerry made a party out of my good news.

The next morning after breakfast Cab sent Drew and Jerry on to their work and he remained behind to talk with me. Cab said to me "I guess you'll be wanting to move on now that you have your divorce and nothing is holding you back." I replied "Nothing could be further from the truth. I love this ranch! Drew, Jerry, and you are like my family." I continued, "I know it's been hard having me here in a small cabin and our privacy is limited. If you want me to leave, I will, but if I were given a choice, I'd never leave." Cab looked satisfied with my answer and didn't reply.

I decided at that moment to be the old Marilyn just once more. I said to Cab in a joking way, "You know there's one way you can keep me on this ranch for the rest of my life and never worry about losing your cook!" Cab looked completely baffled and said to me, "I don't' understand." My answer was, "Marry me, and you will never lose me as long as I live." I continued "In the year that I have known you, you have never said 'No' to anything I have asked for, and I have asked for plenty. I know I've asked for things that you felt was really too much but you always said 'Yes.' Why not say 'Yes' one more time?" A feather would have knocked Cab off his feet. The best he could do was tell me he'd have to think about it. With the end of our conversation, or should I say my proposal, he took his hat and headed out for work.

Later that day, when our noon meal ended, once again Cab lingered in the cabin and sent Drew and Jerry on their way. Cab told me that he'd thought all morning about us getting married and how he'd love to have a son to inherit his ranch and not let all his years of hard work die with him. He was so pleased that I loved the ranch and now he realized all the things I had asked him for only made the ranch a better place. We told Drew and Jerry at supper that night that we had plans to marry and we wanted to change our living arrangements just a bit. Another evening of celebrating ensued. We added a room to the cabin and moved Jerry and Drew to the new addition and that left the cabin for just us. We ordered a double bed from the general store in Emporia. We chose to marry in my little church in Marion so that Jerry and Drew could attend the wedding but still get back to the ranch before night. Cab and I left the church for our one-night honeymoon in Emporia.

During our engagement, Cab had never kissed me or even held my hand so I was a bit nervous about how our wedding night would be. When we got settled into our hotel room for the evening Cab appeared nervous, so I suggested we take our shoes off and lie on the bed so we could rest for a while. Cab slowly pulled off his boots and laid down beside me. He finally got the courage to hold my hand while we talked about our future and about having children. At last, I got the kiss of my dreams and our wedding night became something I will always treasure. The next morning, we had a big breakfast, picked up our new bed from the general store and headed back home.

Life was much the same as before we married, except we had a little more room in the cabin now with Drew and Jerry in their quarters. I still cooked a lot, gardened, made cheese, and now I helped Cab with some of his bookwork for the ranch.

A few months into our marriage I became extremely nauseated and vomited every morning. I was having trouble getting breakfast cooked. The smell would send me running outside to be sick and then I would have to lie down for a while till my nausea passed. Cab ended up doing a lot of the cooking during this time. I finally realized I was pregnant. The rest of my pregnancy was uneventful after my morning sickness improved. Drew made a cradle for the baby. Everyone was so excited about our new addition that was on the way. I prayed for the baby to be a boy since Cab had his heart set on a son.

We lived so far out that getting a doctor to me for delivery would probably be impossible, but we did have a local midwife who was somewhat close to us. Our plan for when my labor started if no one was nearby was for me to shoot the shotgun into the air so that I could get Cab home to help me. Fortunately, I didn't have to do that. Just as we finished our noon meal, my water broke, and Jerry made a fast trip of getting the midwife. My labor was normal, the midwife delivered our son, but I had lost a lot of blood. The midwife was unable to get the bleeding under control, and Jerry quickly went for the doctor racing against time that I wouldn't bleed to death before the doctor arrived. I was in and out of consciousness at this point. I do remember seeing Cab on his knees beside the bed praying to God, "Please don't take her from us." Cab never went to church or showed any signs of Christian belief, but I knew after that day that he did believe.

The doctor arrived late in the evening. He worked with me most of the night and got the bleeding to slow down. I wasn't allowed out of bed for weeks, but I really didn't mind. I was so weak and fainted if I tried to get up. Everyone took turns being my nurse while I struggled to regain my strength. All my suffering was worth it. We had a healthy, baby boy named Marvin Cabot Neely. Marvin was Cab's father's name. Nicknames run in the Neely family and so our baby was nicknamed "Marty." Cab was the proud father for sure, but Uncle Jerry and Uncle Drew were just as proud. Raising Marty became the most important thing in the world to us.

Leland's Story

I was born and raised in Juniper, Georgia just down the road from the Cochran and Hughes farms. There were four of us in the Martin family, my parents, my twin sister, Ida Mae, and me. My family owned the small farm we lived on, but I wouldn't say my father was a farmer. He grew a few crops on the front part of the property near the road so that no one could really see how he made a meager living. His major farm crop was corn for making moonshine whiskey.

As far back as I can remember, Pa was involved in the distillery business. That was his passion in life. The farming he did was to support his real "business" and keep up a good front for the folks in the community. Most days and nights he was down in the woods with his still and his "customers" sampling the latest brew. When Ida Mae and I were small, we liked to play around the still with Pa and his friends, but as we got older, certain events changed our view of the still and Pa. The best way I can put it is when Ida Mae got closer to being a woman than a girl, she had some unpleasant experiences with Pa's drinking companions, and she avoided the still at all cost.

When I was big enough to go hunting and fishing, I knew not to ask Pa to take me. I looked to our neighbors Mr. Hughes and Mr. Cochran to take me. Mr. Cochran adopted me as his "hunting buddy" and made sure I learned the skills of an out-doorsman. None of us were exceptional fishermen, so hunting was our preferred sport.

About four or five of us would make up a hunting party - at least one adult and the rest boys. Mr. Cochran, and sometimes Mr. Hughes, would be the adult in charge. The boys would be Mr. Hughes' three sons, myself and Mr. Cochran's slave boy, Joe.

How Mr. Cochran came to own slave children was a popular subject around Juniper. As the story goes, Mr. Cochran had gone to a lumber yard in Atlanta and was waiting for a wagon of stacked logs to be unloaded when with no warning, the ropes holding the logs suddenly broke; huge logs started rolling off the wagon almost crushing one of the workers. Mr. Cochran risked his life to rush in and pull the man to safety. The owner of the lumber yard was so grateful to Mr. Cochran for saving his employee's life that he gave Mr. Cochran a gift of two, half-grown slave children, Joe and Bessie. The Cochrans never had any children of their own so, in some ways, Joe and Bessie became almost like their children.

My hunting trips helped put food on the table, and my folks liked it when I came home with fresh meat. I went hunting as often as I could – sometimes just to get out of doing chores. Ida Mae would fish with me sometimes, but she wasn't allowed to go often. Ma took in laundry and ironing to help support us, and Ida Mae was expected to stay home and help Ma.

During the war years, I was too young to be a soldier. Most folks in Juniper had strong feelings about the war," It's a rich man's war, and poor folks like us need to stay out of the fighting." As I got into my teen years, I wanted to see more of the world than Juniper, but I didn't see how I could ever break free from the bonds of home. I didn't want to be a farmer, and I certainly didn't want to follow in my father's footsteps. I grew more and more restless. Ida Mae would confide in me that she felt the same way, that there had to be more in life than just barely getting by from one day to the next.

On occasion, I would see Mrs. Woodall, Marilyn's mother, and ask how Marilyn was doing. Ida Mae and Marilyn had been childhood friends. I had heard about Marilyn moving to Kansas with one of her friends from Columbus, and I was always curious about how her life was going living out west. Mrs. Woodall was always glad to tell about Marilyn's progress in making a good life for herself. Ida Mae wanted to go West to find a husband as soon as she heard the men outnumbered the women. That's all she talked about. We both would have jumped at the chance to go West, but we didn't have the money or someone with money to help us as Marilyn did. I knew if I were to plan a trip to Kansas, I'd have to figure out how to get there by my own efforts.

I'll never forget the last conversation I had with Mrs. Woodall. She told me about Marilyn marrying this fella in the freight hauling business and how freight delivery was a thriving business in the West. I couldn't stop thinking about joining up with them and working in the freight business. I started making plans to leave home and head West; I'd have to wait until Spring, and I'd have to walk or, hopefully, get rides with anyone who would take me. I knew it would be tough, but I could fish and hunt to feed myself and fur trade for other supplies. My last step of planning was to ask Mrs. Woodall for Marilyn's address in Kansas.

I kept my plan a secret from everyone except Ida Mae. I trusted her not to say anything to Ma and Pa. I made her promise to act surprised when they discovered I had left home for good. What I had not planned on was Ida Mae's response when I told her I was going West. She wanted to go with me!! I told her that was impossible. It was going to be hard enough for a man to walk to Kansas let alone a woman. She insisted and threatened to tell Ma if I didn't take her with me. I calmed her down by promising to think about it overnight and tell her my decision in the morning.

I had a restless night thinking about such a journey for anyone with no money and only hopes of being able to feed themselves on luck alone. All night I had horrible thoughts about what I would do if one of us got sick and couldn't go on. What would we do? What if Indians or thieves attacked us?

The next morning, we talked through all my concerns, and both agreed it was better to take the risk of a better life in Kansas than to stay in Juniper. Late April became our planned date to leave, so we had about eight weeks to get ready. My only ray of hope in taking Ida Mae with me was that some people might take pity on us if they saw a female traveler. We'd be able to hitch more wagon rides from other travelers than if I was alone. The more I thought about how lonely the trip would be, the more I began to appreciate Ida Mae's willingness to go with me. I had gotten some information from Mrs. Woodall about the roads and trails to travel and where there would be water and no Indians. Ida Mae made a backpack of sorts with the items we'd take with us. It wouldn't be much because we'd need to travel light. We even planned what our "goodbye" note to our parents would say. We planned to leave at dark on the first day so that we'd have a head start on anyone searching for us. We'd have all night to get miles from Juniper before anyone realized we were gone. Maybe in the morning, we'd have good fortune and get a ride on the back of someone's wagon.

It was a full moon on the evening of April 29. Ida Mae and I told our parents "good night, " and we would see them in the morning – nothing could have been further from the truth. When we felt our parents had fallen into deep sleep, we left our "goodbye" note and crept out of the house. Our destination for day one was, Columbus. We had to be ever vigilant for snakes and wild animals on the road, but the bright moon shining down on us made our walk easier. We got a good laugh about the "moonshine" we had - it wasn't the kind anyone could drink. We got to the outskirts of Columbus by daybreak and found an abandoned barn to hide in to catch a few hours of sleep. We were starved and made a meal out of the last of Ma's leftover biscuits we brought with us. Reality set in – where was our next meal coming from and what do we do next?

Ida Mae remembered Mrs. Woodall's telling us about Marilyn's friend, Susan, who lived in Columbus. Before the war, Susan's parents owned a restaurant in Columbus near the cotton mills and the river. Susan was the girl who went to Kansas and later helped Marilyn get to Kansas. Susan had a stepmother living upstairs over the restaurant. We decided to try to find Mrs. Day - maybe she could help us. We wandered around Columbus till we got someone to point us in the direction of the river. As we neared the cotton mills, we found the two-story building with the old restaurant sign still hanging over the door. We climbed the steps to the second story and knocked at the door. When a lady opened the door, we asked, "Are you Mrs. Day?" She said "Yes, " and we proceeded to explain to her who we were. She invited us in and was eager to hear all we knew about how the "Kansas girls" were doing. When we finished our visit, she updated our map as best she could remember of Susan's stage trail and directed us to the right road going North out of Columbus.

From the second day on we walked or hitched rides from folks with room to spare in their wagon. I managed to trap squirrels and rabbits most of the time and keep us fed. Water was plentiful due to the spring rains. Sometimes strangers would share their food with us. We never turned down any work we could find that gave us money for food. Every day was a struggle against the weather, hunger, fatigue, and insects. We walked barefoot as much as we could to save our shoes.

Our clothes became faded, frayed, and dirty, and we both lost a lot of weight. We must have been a sight – two ragged, dirty, near skeletons walking along the dusty roads. The rainy days were the worst. If we could find shelter, we'd just sleep those days away. We had a few scary nights with wild animals and strangers, but for the most part, people treated us with respect or ignored us. The further North we got the harder the journey became. The constant uphill struggle over the mountains and plateaus was exhausting. When we could find an army fort, that was the best. We could rest, and they would give us all the beans we could eat.

We arrived in Council Grove near the end of August. That day seems like a dream now; I was so tired I barely remember getting to the porch of the Hartley Hotel and asking to see Marilyn. Ida Mae fainted on the porch of the hotel probably from hunger. Susan and the Hartleys took us into the hotel and let us stay for several days. Shortly after our arrival, we got the real news about Marilyn, that she had married someone no one approved of and left Council Grove, her whereabouts unknown. Susan let us stay with her until we got settled into jobs and a place to live. Mr. Hartley got Ida Mae a job at the laundry that did the hotel's sheets. I found odd jobs to fill my time, and we rented a room from a modest boarding house.

When I couldn't find any work, I would hang around the hotel and do errands for Mr. Hartley or pass my time with a guest who wanted to talk. I would meet fascinating people, and I was happier than I had ever been in my life. Ida Mae wasn't all that happy though. She hated her job, and I could see why because she had walked a thousand miles just to do the same thing she had been doing in Juniper. She held out hopes of finding a husband and had a few dates, but nothing turned into anything lasting. Ida Mae wasn't an attractive girl, big boned, stringy hair, and plain compared with most women. Even in a town with more men than women, Ida Mae struggled to find a man.

Susan took us under her wing like she'd been our friend all her life and helped us get through some hard cases of homesickness. Council Grove was a thriving town, and because of her work at the hotel, Susan knew about new businesses and influential people coming into town and gladly passed on what she knew. Thanks to Susan, I knew where to look for work, and Ida Mae knew about any single young men coming into town needing to get some laundry done.

We had been living in Council Grove for some time with no news of Marilyn. We knew that Susan didn't want Marilyn to marry Roy Smith and they had a big argument about it. Susan had not heard from Marilyn since she married Roy Smith and left town with him. After months of waiting, Marilyn finally sent Susan a long letter. It started out with an apology over the angry words she had said and that Susan was right about Roy - he was no-good. Marilyn wrote how Roy Smith had left her deserted along the road, stealing her money, mule, and wagon. He had just left her with nothing, probably hoping she'd die. Marilyn's letter also told about the old woman who took her in, how she got a job as a cook on a ranch and was able to get a divorce from Roy Smith. The letter ended with the happy news about her new husband (the man who owned the ranch she worked at), and that she was expecting a baby. The P.S. at the bottom of her letter said that to the best of her knowledge, Roy Smith is still wanted by the sheriff and no word of an arrest. We had a little celebration that evening at the hotel for Marilyn. Even though she wasn't with us, we were glad to hear all was well and she was free from the no-account Roy Smith.

Early one hot and humid morning I was having trouble finding any work, so I went over to the hotel to sit in one of the big rocking chairs on the hotel's front porch and wait for Mr. Hartley to give me an errand. Within a few minutes, a hotel guest arrived by horseback. He was barely able to sit in the saddle. He explained that he was utterly exhausted, that he had been riding most of the night trying to reach Council Grove before stopping to rest. I helped him into the hotel and volunteered to take his horse to the livery stable for him.

When I arrived at the livery, I had to wait for the attendant to finish with a customer ahead of me. The customer was a young man, fancy dressed and I overheard him give his name to the attendant. The name he gave was "Roy Smith." I could feel my heart skip a beat – could that be the scoundrel that Marilyn had married? When Mr. Smith left, I asked the attendant if he'd seen Roy Smith before, and he said he couldn't say. When I left the livery stable, I began searching the saloons for Mr. Smith and found him heavily involved in a poker game in one of the run-down taverns on the outskirts of town. I felt he'd continue gambling for a while and I rushed back to the hotel to tell Mr. Hartley what I had discovered. Mr. Hartley suggested we get the sheriff involved for a possible arrest.

We both went to the sheriff's office only to find him engaged in other business and not able to help us. Mr. Hartley gave me some money and told me to go back to the saloon and keep an eye on him, follow him if I had to. I spent the remainder of the day watching Roy Smith gamble before retiring of all places in the hayloft of the livery stable. I reported back to Mr. Hartley, who gave me more money and told me to continue watching him and that he'd get word to Ida Mae what I was doing. I slept outside the livery door that night so that I'd know if Smith rode out. Smith did ride out early the next morning, and I took Mr. Hartley's horse and proceeded to follow him.

I think he got wise to me following him and I lost his trail near Emporia, Kansas. I located the sheriff at Emporia and explained what I was doing and asked for aid in bringing Roy Smith to justice. The sheriff wasn't a lot of help, but he knew the whole story about Marilyn and other girls Roy Smith had left deserted after robbing them. I telegraphed Mr. Hartley to let him know where I was as well as his horse - I didn't want him to accuse me of being a horse thief.

I stopped in the General Store to inquire if someone matching Roy Smith's description had recently gotten any supplies. The owner had not seen him, but we started talking, and my Georgia accent made him ask me if I knew Marilyn Neely. I said I did that we grew up together back in Georgia. He went on to tell me that the Neely ranch was about a day's ride from Emporia, to head for Marion and I could get directions from there to the Neely ranch. The store owner showed me a partially consumed block of cheese and said, "Miss Marilyn makes this cheese. It's good-try some." The thought of getting to see Marilyn ended all thoughts about Roy Smith, and I made plans to head for Marion at first light.

When morning came, I made my way to the Neely Ranch arriving just before dark. When I knocked on the cabin door, a stern young man answered the door and wanted to know who I was. After I gave my name and the Georgia accent was detected, I was allowed into the cabin. Cab Neely introduced himself as well as Jerry and Drew in a whispering voice explaining that Marilyn had just given birth a few days back and was resting. He told me all about her difficult delivery and how they had almost lost her to complications. After being served a plate of food, I shared with them what I overheard at the livery stable and that I was trailing Roy Smith. Cab remarked that he wished he could take the time to help me hunt him down but he had a sick wife, newborn baby, and a ranch to look after.

When the baby woke up, so did Marilyn. We had a long talk about the journey to Kansas and the folks back in Georgia.

I stayed with them a couple of days and tried to help Cab with some of his chores that had fallen behind when the baby was born. Marilyn asked if Ida Mae would consider staying at the ranch and helping her with the baby and her chores. I felt that Ida Mae would be glad to leave the laundry and spend her days with Marilyn. I had taken a liking to Cab and liked being around the ranch. We all decided that I should go back to Emporia and send a telegram to Ida Mae telling her that Marilyn needed help. I waited only a short while when Ida Mae answered my telegram back saying she would be on the next stage. I waited in Emporia for her, and in three days the stagecoach arrived with Ida Mae and Susan!

Ida Mae didn't want to make the trip alone, and Susan wanted to see Marilyn and the baby. Susan's visit was short, but the girls made the most of the time they had together. I drove Susan back to Emporia in the wagon with Mr. Hartley's horse tied behind. Susan and the horse took the stage back to Council Grove, but Ida Mae stayed behind.

Ida Mae was a Godsend to all of us but especially to Marilyn. She came ready to help and in no rush to go back to Council Grove.

Ida Mae's Story

Leland and I are fraternal twins, and he's the oldest by a few minutes. Some folks don't believe we're twins because we don't look alike at all. Ma probably never saw a doctor before we were born and could not have known she was going to have twins. To have two babies born on the same day must have been quite a shock to our parents. All our lives we heard how difficult it was to manage two infants at one time. Their remarks about raising twins didn't seem to bother Leland, but it did me. I took the complaining personally. Their comments made me feel that they regretted that I had been born and they would have been happy if our birthday was just Leland's.

Leland and I grew up in Juniper, Georgia and shared a bond of dislike for our parents. There's no polite way to put it; Pa was a drunk. His motivation for getting up in the morning was to check on his latest brew at the still and then sample it. He came by his ways honest since that's the way most of Pa's folks were. The Martins were afraid of anything ambitious. Hard work was taboo. Even with Pa's laziness and drinking, he was easier to get along with than Ma. Leland and I would entertain ourselves after supper with a game we made up - betting on the exact time Pa would drink himself into a stupor and pass out.

Ma was hard to get along with, always cold and bitter, with no compassion for anyone. I think her childhood made her that way. Ma was the oldest of five children, and when she was around twelve years old, her mother died. Her Pa made her quit school and be responsible for her younger siblings. As if that weren't enough, she had all the cooking and washing duties as well. Ma didn't get to be a child long enough. She married my Pa when she was quite young only to realize she had married a hopeless alcoholic. Then her firstborn turned out to be the double work of twins, Leland and me. She had a life of bad luck, and her way of dealing with all those disappointments was bitterness.

Critical words and beatings with a limb from the Sweet Gum tree were the only parental attention we received. The verbal abuse for me and the beatings for Leland. Leland would fight back and take up for himself, but I never had the courage. Despite all this, we did our best in school and managed to have a few friends.

As I got older and started to develop, I had some unpleasant experiences when I'd be around Pa's still and his "customers." The men sitting around the still out in the woods would insist that I come "visit" with them. "Visits" meant that I was forced to sit on their laps, and they'd put their hands on me in inappropriate places. Pa would never tell them to stop! He'd just laugh and say I was good for business because they would stay and drink more if they had some entertainment. When I told Ma, what was going on at the still, she got infuriated with me. She said it was my responsibility to make those men behave. Her last words on the subject were, "You must be enjoying it, or you would have put a stop to it." At first, I was devastated by what she said, and then I began to feel ashamed. Ma made me feel like it was my fault. I knew I wasn't pretty to look at on the outside and now I must be "no good" on the inside as well. Instead of helping me, Ma continued to send me to the still to get Pa home at night or to take supper down to the "customers."

I told Leland what was happening and he confronted Pa. Leland was just a half-grown boy, and there was nothing he could do to help me. Pa even warned him to "keep his mouth shut, " or we'd both be in serious trouble. That's about the time Leland and I started to talk about running away. We had to just wait for the right opportunity. When we heard about Marilyn and her friend from Columbus going to Kansas, we wanted to leave home to join Marilyn in Kansas. This was what we'd been waiting for.

For us to be so young and knowing so little about the ways of the world, it's a miracle we survived the journey to Kansas. Just getting to Kansas was not the end of our suffering, we had not prepared for how hard life in Council Grove would be. Lots of help from Susan and the Hartleys kept us alive those first weeks.

I should have appreciated the laundry job Mr. Hartley arranged for me, but I hated it. I consoled myself that it was a paycheck till something better came along. Working in the laundry was better than some of the stories about girls making it to Kansas with no money and ending up working in saloons and brothels to keep from starving. Most days I was so exhausted from my laundry job that I went to bed right after supper not leaving me anytime for socializing. We managed to eat and have a roof over our heads, but our money was tight. Leland and I pooled our money and shared a small room at the boarding house to stretch every dollar we had.

Not finding Marilyn in Council Grove when we first arrived was a big disappointment, and even more discouraging was finding out that Marilyn and Susan were no longer on speaking terms. I was afraid we'd never find Marilyn because we had so little information about where she'd gone. When homesickness would overtake us, Susan would do her best to be the friend to us we had expected Marilyn to be. One Sunday afternoon she rented a buggy and took us out to see Joe and Bessie. That was a wonderful day.

A long wished-for letter addressed to Susan finally came to the hotel. It was an apology letter from Marilyn. Susan read the letter to us telling all of Marilyn's news (good and bad). Susan wrote back the same day with her news. There had been so much time between Susan's and Marilyn's argument; we had made our journey from Georgia to Kansas and Marilyn had no knowledge of any of this. The letter stirred up feelings of deep friendship and made us want a reunion.

One hot, summer afternoon, I was working in the laundry and looked up to see Mr. Hartley wanting to talk with me. He had a serious look on his face that scared me until he shared that Leland had overheard a man at the livery stable say his name was Roy Smith. Mr. Hartley asked, "Do you remember who Roy Smith is?" I replied, "Yes - the scoundrel that deserted Marilyn in the woods." Mr. Hartley told me that Leland had volunteered to follow him, even if it meant following him out of town. He added, "Leland is the perfect man for the job. He can recognize Roy Smith, but to Smith, Leland is just another stranger. Leland plans to stay on his trail and hopefully have him arrested." When Mr. Hartley took his leave, he promised to keep me posted and to be patient and wait.

Being patient and waiting wasn't easy but it paid off. Several days went by with no word from Leland other than he was in Emporia and had spoken with the sheriff there. When I got a telegram from Leland asking me to help Marilyn and the baby, I quit my job and started packing. Susan and I bought stagecoach tickets and left town for Emporia.

Leland waited for our stage to arrive in Emporia, and after a long, bumpy wagon ride we arrived about dark at the Neely ranch. Susan could only stay one night, so I let Marilyn and Susan visit as much as possible. I was hoping I would have plenty of time with Marilyn in the coming days, as I had my heart set on staying at the ranch for a long, long time. The next morning came all too soon. We witnessed a sad and tearful parting as these two grown women, friends since they were little girls, said goodbye.

Cab wouldn't let us talk about the Roy Smith news around Marilyn because he felt she was still too weak from her complicated childbirth. He wasn't going to let Roy Smith hurt her ever again.

The days went by so fast, and I tried my best to do a good job for Cab and Marilyn so that they wouldn't send me back to my old laundry job. I wanted them to ask me to stay on permanently.

Hours of time alone in the cabin gave Marilyn and me time to catch up on our lives and for me to get all the details on Roy Smith and their brief marriage. Looking back now, I realize that the details Marilyn gave me were really her testimony on how she came to be a born-again Christian. Marilyn summed up her experience with Roy Smith as something bad that God turned into something good. Marilyn admitted, "I would never have the faith I have now if I hadn't experienced hurt and fear when Roy Smith deserted me." She had been so down on her luck that the only direction she could look was up to God.

Marilyn had a way of making me feel good about myself. She always complimented me, and I slowly began to develop some confidence and self-worth. We had Bible study almost every night, and I would always ask her to read verses that told how much God loved us. Marilyn's faith was not the condemning kind like the church I went to as a child back in Juniper. Marilyn's God was all about love and salvation. Our Bible study began to lead me out of a life of condemnation. I was a child of

God and precious in His sight. I had to face a choice - live my life for Christ or continue listening to the lies in my head put there by my parents. I was baptized in Marilyn's church and made my faith top priority. God blessed me with happiness and peace.

Leland didn't want any part of our Bible study or church attendance. We tried many times to talk to him, witness to him, but our efforts fell on deaf ears. Leland was prideful - simple as that. He was the opposite of me always nice-looking, strong, talented, outgoing, made friends easily, and could talk his way out of most anything. I came to be thankful for my weaknesses without them I would never have looked to God. I began to pity Leland because he never wanted a spiritual life. He never got to experience the love and peace that I felt.

Marilyn and Jerry had kept the cheese business going until the baby was born, but Marilyn's difficult delivery had stopped all production. She was too weak to do any heavy work. My new job was to help Jerry, and I was eager to learn the cheese business. As Marilyn's substitute, I worked side by side with Jerry seven days a week. We became the best of friends. Our friendship led to marriage despite the difference in our ages. We loved each other, and that's all that mattered. Cab added onto the cabin to give us a small bedroom for ourselves.

On a cold winter night, a little over two years into our marriage, Jerry died peacefully in his sleep. We picked a beautiful spot under a cottonwood tree for his final resting place. That place was later named the Neely Cemetery. I mourned for a long time after Jerry's passing.

The Indian Girls' School

Leland felt obligated to stay on with Cab and Marilyn after Jerry's death but was looking for an opportunity to leave. His desire to move on was almost overwhelming, but at the same time, his guilty feelings caused him to put his ambitions aside for a while. Leland did not want to leave Ida Mae while she was grieving plus Cab was short-handed now that Drew had taken over Jerry's duties. To top it off, everyone was in mourning over the loss of Jerry, and his leaving would just make matters worse.

Ida Mae was looking for something in her life to fill the void left by Jerry's death. One morning she was reading the Emporia newspaper when she spotted an article about Reverend Faulkner in Council Grove opening a school for Indian girls. His school was to focus on teaching them Christianity, English, and a vocation. He was still short of qualified teachers and was seeking more applicants. He was looking for women in good standing in the community, single, strong in the Christian faith, and willing to be a live-in teacher. The description of the school intrigued Ida Mae. The only skill she possessed that would be of interest to the school would be her knowledge of cheesemaking. Marilyn encouraged her to apply and reassured her that if she wasn't happy at the school, she was welcome to come back home.

Reverend Faulkner was pleased with Ida Mae's application and was immediately accepted as a teacher in the Department of Food Preparation. When Ida Mae learned that the teaching staff, could board their horses at the school, Cab gave Jerry's horse to Ida Mae. Now with the gift of the horse, she had the freedom to go where she pleased and stay in touch with friends.

Leland and Ida Mae set out for Council Grove a few days early so they'd have time to visit with friends before Ida Mae started her teaching job. They stayed at the Hartley Hotel, but Leland became bored with the girl-talk by the second evening and decided to find something more interesting at one of the saloons in town. Leland was always short on money, so he headed for the less expensive saloons on the edge of town. The excitement and adventure he was looking for waited just inside the saloon's swinging doors. Upon entering the doorway, his eyes fell directly on Roy Smith sitting at one of the poker tables.

Smith was oblivious to everyone around him. Leland ordered a beer and tried to act natural, but all the while wanting to make a run for the sheriff's office. Leland finally felt he could make an exit unnoticed and quickly ran for the sheriff's office. The sheriff was working late!! Not taking time for any pleasantries as he threw open the office door, he blurted out, "I just saw Roy Smith in the Lacey Garter Saloon!" Sheriff Oliver looked up at Leland and quietly answered him "I know." Sheriff Oliver went on to tell Leland that he'd been keeping an eye on him and that he suspected the opening of the Indian Girls' School was probably the reason he was in town. Those young girls or the teachers would be easy pickings for someone like Roy Smith. The sheriff added that if Roy Smith kidnapped one of those girls or harmed them in any way it would end any hope of the Indians staying on peaceful terms. The situation was serious.

Leland asked, "What are you going to do?" Sheriff Oliver replied, "I'm keeping an eye on him but I am just one man, and

I can't watch him 24 hours a day. I could use some help if you're interested, I'll deputize you tonight, and there's some pay that comes with the job." Leland didn't think twice replying, "I'm your man."

The sheriff said, "I want to be absolutely sure that I'm watching the right man. You told me you overheard him say his name was Roy Smith but you've never had any dealings with him, is that right?" "Yes, that's right," answered Leland. "Anybody can say their name is such and such and that doesn't make it true. I need positive identification that the man in the saloon is Roy Smith and the only people in town that know him for sure is Susan Day and the Hartleys. The problem is Smith knows them and would run like a jackrabbit if they came anywhere near him."

Leland asked, "What about the livery stable attendant?" The sheriff replied "I asked him. He said he sees so many people he just can't remember him. No help there."

Sheriff Oliver was quiet for a few minutes and then began to speak, "We need someone working at the school, a woman, who knows what Roy Smith looks like and the sound of his voice but is unfamiliar to Smith. I'm sorry to say we need a woman for this job. It irks me that we got to use our women folks like this, but I don't see any other way. I'd like to have a teacher help us keep an eye out for Smith - he'd never suspect them. I haven't told anyone but you and the headmistress about my plan. The fewer people that know, the less chance Smith will get wind of my scheme."

Leland got so excited, almost to the point of not being clear when he tried to speak. "I have the perfect teacher for you – my sister, Ida Mae! I just brought her to town to start work at the school as a teacher. The only thing is, she doesn't know what Roy Smith looks like either but I know she'd do it. Marilyn Neely is one of our best friends."

"What a stroke of luck," a smiling Sheriff Oliver replied. "Now we need to figure out a way for her to see and hear Smith but remain anonymous to him." The men passed ideas back and forth, but no solution seemed to be foolproof. Finally, the sheriff suggested a plan, "I've made every saloon owner in town drill a peephole into a wall so that I can go into their stock rooms and look through the peephole to see who's in their saloon – it's been a great help to me over the years. Here is what I'm proposing. What about Ida Mae and the headmistress go into the saloon when Smith is in there gambling, have the women approach several of the men in the saloon asking for help moving some heavy equipment - ask for some freight haulers. Remember Smith's lie is that he's in the freight business. Let's see if he takes the bait. That way both ladies get to see and hear him. We'll have you, Susan, Mr. Hartley, and me hide out in the saloon's store-room looking through the peephole and confirm which man is Roy Smith. After the ladies have had a good look at Smith, I am going to leave the storeroom, enter the saloon, and say to them, Ladies, this is no place for you. You need to move on." He added "I've got one concern. I don't trust the barkeeper because Smith's a good customer and I don't know where his loyalty lies. That leaves all of us to sneak out of the stockroom unseen."

Leland agreed with the plan and organized everyone. All parties accepted that they could be facing embarrassment and trespassing charges if the barkeeper saw them. The day came for the execution of their scheme, and good luck was with them - it went without a hitch. The group met at the school when the charade was over to review the success of their evening. The consensus was that Smith had taken the bait about the freight business and now everyone could identify him!

The next morning brought in a well-dressed, young man at the school office to finish discussing the freight business that had been interrupted by the sheriff the evening before. The headmistress summoned Ida Mae explaining that Ida Mae could give him the details he needed. Ida Mae immediately came downstairs and graciously met with Smith. She played her part well, giving him dimensions and weight of various machines used in the school. Smith listened and made notes. Ida Mae mentally prepared herself for whatever she had to do to bring Smith to justice. She made a forward remark to Smith, asking him to have lunch at the school with her so they'd have more time to work. Smith accepted the invitation and began his flirting with Ida Mae. While all this took place, the headmistress had gotten word to Sheriff Oliver and Leland that Smith was on the school grounds with Ida Mae. Smith had no idea he was under constant surveillance.

The next day a letter from the sheriff in Alma, Kansas was delivered to Sheriff Oliver. Leland had never seen Sheriff Oliver so emotional and close to tears so he waited quietly in the office till Sheriff Oliver could speak. Leland was curious about the letter and the small scrap of cloth he held so tenderly in his other hand. In a few minutes, Sheriff Oliver said, "Let me read you this letter. It's heartbreaking to imagine what this young woman went through."

The letter said:

Sherriff Oliver

I have reason to believe a man by the name of Roy Smith might be in or passing through Council Grove. I felt it best not to telegram you as I want to keep this information in the hands of law officials only. This Smith character is suspected in the kidnapping of a young girl here in Alma. Her name is Jenny Belk. Her parents reported her missing about a year ago. A way station worker found her

unconscious behind a way station just north of Denver.
When the way station employee got her inside, she came
to long enough to tell him her name (Jenny Belk) and
that she had been kidnapped by a man named Roy Smith
of Council Grove. This Smith took her to Georgetown,
Colorado (a mining camp north of Denver) and sold her
to a brothel house there, and rode off leaving her. She
escaped on foot after months of captivity and made her
way to the way station where she was found. She died a
few hours after being found. Her condition was reported
to be pitiful - just skin and bone. Her last request was
to tear a piece of material from her dress and mail it
along with a letter to her parents to let them know what
happened to her and give them something to remember
her by. The folks at the way station were so moved by
her story that they took clothes from their belongings for
her to be buried in and insisted the dress she died in be
mailed to her parents. The Belks have identified the dress
as belonging to their daughter. Please be on the lookout
for this scoundrel. It would be a pleasure to see this ani-
mal swinging from a rope. I am enclosing a scrap of her
dress in case you need it for court in the future.

Sincerely

Jake Edmond
Sheriff of Alma, Kansas

Leland was just as moved by the letter as the sheriff had
been. The determination to charge Smith was more fervent
than ever! Smith was more dangerous than anyone realized.
Marilyn had been lucky. Roy Smith had only taken her money
and possessions.

The next plan Sheriff Oliver had was more dangerous than the first. He wanted to wait for Smith to make his move and he felt that an unlucky night of poker might just push Smith into his "freight business." Smith would be ready to make his "easy money" by kidnapping an innocent female and selling her. Everyone was waiting for the fate of the cards to drive Smith to desperation for money. Days later they got word that Smith had lost a lot of money gambling the night before and was flat broke. Using the sheriff's plan, Ida Mae (under the watchful eye of Leland) made a point to tell Smith how unhappy she was as a teacher at the school. Ida Mae complained about how hard it was to work for the strict schoolmistress, and she wanted to leave the school but didn't have anywhere to go and no family or friends to turn to for help. Smith believed her, saying under his breath "This one is gonna be easy." Smith suggested a ride and picnic on the prairie where they could talk without fear of anyone overhearing them. Ida Mae agreed and even suggested her horse needed the exercise, and with that, the picnic plans went into motion.

Brother Leland was beside himself with worry over the thought of Ida Mae riding out of town with a known kidnapper. This picnic was too risky, but he understood it was the only way to be sure of a conviction if Smith was caught red-handed. With Marilyn's testimony, the Jenny Belk letter, and this attempted kidnap, no judge or jury would let Roy Smith go free.

Ida Mae and Roy Smith rode out of town with a picnic basket tied to Roy's saddle just as they had planned it. The picnic took place under a shady cottonwood tree, and it was a pleasant outing until Roy Smith suddenly changed into a monster. Without warning his face suddenly turned mean and angry. He grabbed Ida Mae's arms as tight as he could while tying her hands. Ida Mae's protests and screams lead to being gagged with Smith's bandana. He forced her onto her horse. Ida Mae cooperated truly afraid for her life. The two rode off at a fast gallop and Smith was holding the reins to both horses. They rode hard for several hours before stopping for the night and making camp. Ida Mae tried to guess what was going on in Smith's mind. She figured he wanted as many miles as possible between them and Council Grove. Leland and Sheriff Oliver followed them but had to watch from a distance – praying nothing happened to Ida Mae before they could get to her. If Smith suspected anything, all bets were off.

The next morning, Sheriff Oliver remarked, "Looks like Smith isn't in a big hurry from what I've observed at their campsite. I'm real thankful for that." Just after sunrise, Smith saddled up both horses, and they rode out with Smith once again in control of both horses' reins. Ida Mae had not eaten since the picnic and had only had sips of water; she was weak and tired. Smith had taken rations, but he was the only one eating and drinking. After an hour or so of riding, Ida Mae began to slump in her saddle with her face downcast, riding just a few feet behind Smith. The quiet ride instantly ceased when Ida Mae screamed, "Snake! " Her horse immediately moved to the right of the snake while Smith's horse overreacted by rearing up causing him to take a hard fall to the ground and lose his grip on the horses' reins. His sudden impact with the ground caused the rattlesnake to bite Smith on his left forearm. Ida Mae seized the moment to gain her freedom when she saw Smith trying to tie a makeshift tourniquet around his arm and suck the blood from the snakebite. With no bridle rein to guide her horse, she grabbed a handful of the horse's mane, using it to turn her horse in the direction of Council Grove and hopefully Leland and Sheriff Oliver. Smith didn't pursue her. He was too busy trying to save his life from the snakebite.

Leland and Sheriff Oliver had witnessed the snake incident and lost no time getting to Ida Mae. After seeing she was unharmed, they rode up to where Smith was standing all alone – his horse had galloped off after the snake scare. Sheriff Oliver placed him under arrest for kidnapping while Leland went after the loose horse. This time Smith was the one being hand-tied and forced into his saddle. The long ride back to Council Grove started.

Sheriff Oliver figured Smith wouldn't live to see the jail, most times death came a few hours after a snakebite. Leland even joked about the snake probably died from being exposed to a scoundrel like Smith. The ride back to Council Grove was long and exhausting. Everyone but Smith opted for short rest periods and to keep going so they could arrive at the jail late that night.

Smith was put to bed in his jail cell, all the while screaming in pain and agony from the snakebite. The doctor was summoned to the jail, and a brief examination was performed. The doctor commented "His fingers are cold, probably no blood supply and the necrosis of the tissue has started. If he's still alive in the morning, we'll need to amputate his arm. I gave him a strong pain sedative – hopefully, he'll stay quiet so you all can get some sleep tonight."

The next morning found a very much alive and complaining Roy Smith locked away in his jail cell. When the doctor made his visit to see if he had a patient or not, he was surprised to see Smith had survived the night. He proceeded to examine Smith's arm and again stressed the need to amputate as soon as possible. The amputation would require two strong men to hold Smith down during the surgery. Leland volunteered with delight to assist in the operation and secured the service of a town drunk as the second man to hold down Roy Smith. The second "volunteer" received a promise of the rest of the whiskey bottle that Smith wouldn't drink before he passed out from the surgery. Needless to say, Smith only received sparse sips of whiskey to ease his pain.

Weeks passed by, Roy Smith healed from his amputation and survived a deadly snakebite with not much to look forward to but a trial that would find him guilty of kidnapping. Roy Smith was not aware that the sheriff had other charges other than the abduction of Ida Mae. He had lost his left hand and part of his arm, his fancy clothes and boots were taken from him and sold to pay the doctor for saving his life. He was given a prisoner uniform for clothes and moccasins for shoes. His attorney took a liking to his horse and swapped his legal fee for his horse.

The sheriff began to get his charges for trial ready. The charges so far were Ida Mae's kidnapping, the Jenny Belk letter, and de-position from the way station operator - but Sheriff Oliver was a superstitious man and wanted three charges brought against Smith. He never forgot Marilyn's story. What haunted him about her story was not her survival but the stolen mule and wagon – if only there were proof that Smith was a horse thief, that would see him put away for life or hanged. He got more information from Susan and Marilyn about the mule and wagon that Smith sold the day he deserted Marilyn near Emporia.

Sheriff Oliver wrote to Mrs. Woodall (Marilyn's mother) asking for more information about the purchase of the mule and wagon used by her daughter to reach Kansas. He explained that they had been stolen and he needed to know the names on the bill of sale for the mule. Mrs. Woodall wrote back:

Sheriff Oliver

A dear family friend, the late Mr. Hughes, came by the mule from a Union officer under the "40 acres and

*a mule" law that was passed after the war ended. Mr.
Hughes took Joe Cochran, our neighbor's slave, to get his
free mule that the law had promised to freed slaves. A
Yankee officer signed over the mule to Joe. The wagon
was given to Marilyn (my daughter) and Joe. Mr. Hughes
let them think they had purchased the mule and wagon
with Susan Day's money when, in fact, all of it was given
to them. I don't have a bill of sale as such except the paper
the Union officer gave Mr. Hughes the day him and Joe
went to get the mule.*

> *Sincerely*
> *Mrs. Woodall*

Sheriff Oliver put down Mrs. Woodall's letter and said to
himself, "So, Roy Smith stole a Union army mule from a freed
slave. That should help me get his third charge."

Sheriff Oliver asked for a court date after receiving Mrs.
Woodall's letter. The judge heard all the charges and evidence.
Mr. Nolan, Joe's employer, testified in court that the mule was
never returned to his farm after Joe let Roy Smith use the mule
and wagon under the pretense that he was borrowing it. The
case with Ida Mae was clear-cut – Smith had been caught with
Ida Mae's hands tied and had been seen forcing her to go with
him. The jury then heard the reading of Jenny Belk's letter while
the scrap of material from her dress was passed through the jury
box. The trial lasted part of an afternoon, and the jury returned a
guilty verdict on all three charges in less than an hour. The judge
sentenced Roy Smith to life imprisonment at the penitentiary
in Lansing, Kansas. The citizens of Council Grove were in high
spirits and celebrated that justice had prevailed.

The Final Years

The front page of the Council Grove newspaper read "Twins Help Sheriff Capture Fugitive." Roy Smith was front-page news, and the town folks continued to talk about him even after his transfer to prison. His scandalous actions made for sensational newspaper reporting and Leland continued to enjoy the limelight as the hero brother that helped Sheriff Oliver rescue his sister.

When Leland's popularity began to wane, the urge to move on overtook him, and he eventually left Council Grove to explore more of the West. Ida Mae received a few letters from him, but as the years went by, the letters became fewer and fewer and eventually stopped. Ida Mae never received official word of his passing, but she knew he was dead – probably something that only twins would know about one another. Over the years many prayers had been offered up for Leland, and finally, with great sorrow, Ida Mae accepted that her brother had remained the prideful and self-centered man he'd always been.

Ida Mae never enjoyed the attention that the Smith arrest and trial brought. She was eager to get back to a normal life and was thankful that life in the school was a bit secluded from the prying public, always wanting more details about her ordeal. The Indian Girls' School closed after the third term which was no surprise to anyone. Enrollment was down to just a few girls and no longer of interest to politicians. Ida Mae found herself without a job and was planning to return to the Neely ranch. Reverend Faulkner approached her about becoming a missionary at an Indian school in Nebraska. She accepted the challenge and moved on to missionary work with numerous Indian nations over the remainder of her life. She lived a long life and peacefully died in her sleep – just like the love of her life, Jerry. Marilyn had Ida Mae's body brought back to the ranch and buried her beside Jerry.

Before Ida Mae died, she retold a family story that Susan and Marilyn knew very well, but the event had a moral message that everyone seemed to overlook. The moral message was - that one small Christian act could change the lives of many. Everyone knew the details, but it was Ida Mae who recognized the moral value of the event. Her re-telling was:

"As far as I can remember, Leland never wrote a letter to our parents in all the years we lived in Kansas, but I finally wrote my parents one letter. I wrote them while I was working in the laundry just shortly after we arrived in Council Grove – I was so homesick that day. In the letter, I let them know we were well and had found work. I later learned that my parents had tried to write to us after we left Juniper but we never received their letter. Our visit with Susan's step-mother, Catherine Day, in Columbus that first day we ran away had caused Mrs. Day to become suspicious that our parents didn't know where we were. Mrs. Day felt obligated to get in touch with them. She didn't know our folks, so she contacted Marilyn's mother. She knew Mrs. Woodall would know the Martins. That one thought of concern for the Martins – total strangers to her - led two old friends to renew their friendship. Catherine Day was struggling financially, and Mrs. Woodall was suffering from loneliness. If Mrs. Day had not reached out to help a stranger, Mrs. Day and

Mrs. Woodall would have continued to live in need. I believe God blessed both of those women that day."

The blessing that Ida Mae believed had occurred was the start of a boarding house in Columbus that Mrs. Day and Mrs. Woodall ran. The mills in Columbus were making a slow comeback and men wanted to live near their jobs. Catherine Day still lived upstairs in the two-story building that had once been the Day's Restaurant. With financial aid from Mrs. Woodall (she had received a small inheritance when Mr. Hughes died), they rented the first floor and converted the old restaurant into boarding rooms for the mill hands and reopened the kitchen to serve meals to their guests. The D & W (Day & Woodall) Boarding House gave Mrs. Day the additional money she desperately needed and gave Mrs. Woodall the companionship she needed.

The blessings did not stop there - the working men received a place to live and a chance to witness the Christian faith of those two women.

Susan continued living and working at the hotel until the Hartleys passed away. Mr. Hartley was the first to pass after suffering a stroke. The restaurant and the hotel proved to be too much for Mrs. Hartley to manage, so she leased out the restaurant and operated the hotel as a boarding house. Susan stayed on with Mrs. Hartley through the boarding house years until Mrs. Hartley died. Relatives of Mr. Hartley inherited the hotel, but they had no interest in it and sold it. The once popular hotel became a declining boarding house and remained Susan's residence. To fill her time after Mrs. Hartley's passing, Susan pursued more nursing duties around Council Grove and made frequent visits to Marilyn and Ida Mae. Susan lived a great many years and died from pneumonia. Her last request was to be buried in the Neely Cemetery.

Joe and Bessie spent their best years working for the Nolans. They never considered homesteading or leaving the Nolans because they felt secure with them. There were always rumors about freed slaves being taken advantage of, and Joe and Bessie knew they had a limited education and might be easily taken. So, they decided to stay where they knew they were safe. The Roy Smith incident with Marilyn caused them to fear strangers even more. Their memories of watching every dollar during their travel to Kansas made them afraid of not having their needs met, and they saved their money faithfully. They occasionally splurged at the general store on clothes, shoes, and candy and eventually saved enough to replace the stolen mule and wagon that Roy Smith took from them.

Marilyn summed up a lifelong marriage to Cab this way, "In all my married life with Cab he never told me he loved me. I knew he did by his actions and that was enough for me." Marty was their only child, just like Susan and Marilyn had been their parents' only child. When folks would ask Cab if he wanted more children, Cab would jokingly say, "I couldn't live through another childbirth."

Cab invested everything they had into their ranch and Marilyn pursued her little cheese business. Marilyn liked to look back at her youth as a sharecropper's daughter and compare herself with what she had now. She enjoyed the satisfaction of knowing that her son would never know what it was like to be a sharecropper on someone else's property.

Cab and Drew passed away on the same day. They both came in sick one night with flu-like symptoms and remained sick for days before they died. Marilyn buried them alongside Jerry and Ida Mae.

Marilyn had no choice but to take on the responsibility of the family business. Marty was a teenager not mature enough to handle a ranch, so she sent for her lifelong friends, Joe and

Bessie, to come if possible. They gladly came to Marilyn's rescue. Joe took over the care of the livestock while Bessie took charge of the kitchen. As Bessie and Marilyn aged, the cheese making business became more work than they could do and they were forced to stop production. Joe and Bessie remained with Marilyn for the rest of their lives. They were laid to rest in the Neely Cemetery.

In her later years, Marilyn suffered from numerous dental problems and infections. From her sickbed, she reminded Marty to never forget what he was taught all his life - "That our Lord is an amazing God that loves to bless His own and that in spite of all the bad things that happen to us, God turns those bad experiences into our good." She told him stories about the hardships that Joe, Bessie, and she had endured from Georgia to Kansas and how it was a miracle they survived the journey. She expressed her regret that she didn't have the faith back then that she did now. She often asked Marty to read aloud her favorite Bible verse:

Proverbs 16:9. In their hearts, humans plan their course, but the Lord establishes their steps.

Marty asked, "Why is that your favorite, Mama?" Marilyn replied, "I've always thought that verse described my journey to Council Grove and my life in Kansas."

Marilyn lived long enough to see Marty a grown man before her passing. She was laid to rest in the Neely Cemetery beside Cab. Marty inherited the Neely Ranch and was the first generation of Woodall descendants to own his land.

Marilyn's Favorite Recipes

Venison Soup

2 meaty bones from either the neck, ribs or hindquarters
4 to 5 cups of water
salt & pepper
2 beaten eggs
dash of ground nutmeg

Simmer meaty bone in salt water for 2 hours. Remove bones and strain liquid. Add remaining ingredients slowly and stir constantly, then simmer a few more minutes. Makes about 4 cups of broth.

Slapjacks

Mix flour, sugar, and water (add yeast if you have) to make a paste. Fry in hot fat or lard.

Brunswick Stew

8 - 10 pounds of meat, cut into small pieces
4 cups of peeled tomatoes
3 onions, diced
2 green peppers, diced
¾ cup vinegar
¼ cup sugar or molasses
1 cup water
¼ cup flour
salt & pepper
½ teaspoon turmeric (add more if needed)
hot peppers diced
2 cups corn

Combine all ingredients except flour and water. Make a paste with flour and water, add to other ingredients. Cook at a simmer until corn is done. Makes about 15 servings.

Ida Mae's Bible Verses

Below are some of Ida Mae's favorite Bible verses that she committed to memory. She repeatedly said these verses for years, and God's word healed the little girl inside her. His Word washed away the feelings of being worthless and the shame that she had carried all of her childhood. She was rewarded with peace and self-esteem.

Genesis 1:27 So God created mankind in his own image, in the image of God he created him; male and female he created them.

Psalm 139:13-14 For you created my inmost being; you knit me together in my mother's womb. I praise you because I am fearfully and wonderfully made; your works are wonderful, I know that full well.

Romans 8:1 Therefore, there is now no condemnation for those who are in Christ Jesus, because through Christ Jesus the law of the Spirit who gives life has set you free from the law of sin and death.

Ephesians 2:10 For we are God's handiwork, created in Christ Jesus to do good works, which God prepared in advance for us to do.